Zaid was born in Pakistan. His parents moved to England when he was a year old. This is his first book of short stories. He has lived and worked in many countries but England is where he is at home.

His special thanks are to Ali Ekber Ucar who inspired him to write in the first place. Thanks are also due to Catherine Drayton and Baki Erdal for their encouragement.

GW00633320

THE END OF THE WORLD

&

OTHER STORIES

Zaid S Sethi

First published in Hungary by the author 2009,
Wesselenyi u.16, Budapest 1077, Hungary
zaidsethi@gmail.com

ISBN 978-963-06-6795-1

Printed and bound by Prime Rate Kft.
(www.primerate.hu)
Budapest, Hungary 2009

For Ruby, my best friend, with eternal gratitude and in memory of my parents for the life they gave me.

CONTENTS

The End of the World

I

The world came to an end on the day that you called to say that you cared. I had waited so long to hear a word from you that I could believe in. Anything, any lie that would restore my faith in the possibility to dream again, but nothing happened. And then you rang to say that you cared. It wasn't fair. I had waited so long and when I had lost all hope you rang to say you cared. All those rivers of tears that I had saved in memory of you had washed away any hope of being with you, with the one person in the world that I loved and with whom I could spend the rest of eternity and never have a moment of regret. You didn't come to me. You stayed away through all those moments when I needed you so desperately and then, when I had no hope left of ever seeing you in my arms again, you called to say you cared.

I screamed until the neighbours rushed over to see what had happened. They thought I was dying but it was worse. The world had ended but I was still alive. Alive to hear the crashing of mountains, the tearing up of rain forests that had so long protected the earth from creeping deserts and your voice, a voice that I would have leapt off the ledge to hear again, tore at my heart. They heard my screams, those unnecessary neighbours who would not leave me to die. I saw them all around me and yet all I heard was the silence, the silence that marked the end of the world. I didn't hear a sound.

The silence was painful. I tried so hard to remember hearing what the neighbours said they heard but I heard nothing.

I don't know what love is. I have read about it but that doesn't mean much. The words that I have seen painted across countless pages seemed common place with what I felt. No-one described what I went through. I thought I loved you.

I remember once, getting off the train at Euston I sat on a bench on the platform and cried my heart out. Passengers walked past me. I saw them through the tears but no-one came up to me and said 'Don't cry.' It would have been different for you.

II

It was spring almost two years ago. The world was a richer place, then. Donald was two years old. We went for a walk in the park. It was cold and you complained that it was too cold to take him out. We were still practicing being parents. Two years and we still couldn't accept that we had nothing to prove to each other. Neither was the better parent. I couldn't feed him properly, or give him a bath. You accused me of not loving him. It hurt me when you said that. I loved him as my own flesh and blood and yet that didn't mean anything to you. I loved him. I know you did but I loved him too. You had waited so long for this child. Years of hope, of trying without either pleasure or success had left us exhausted.

You didn't want to adopt and finally when you agreed that we should at least try to see what would happen if we registered with the adoption agency I was to blame again. I had not realised that mixed race parents were not suitable. They didn't say that exactly but when they said that it would be hard to find a child that would be suitable I knew what they meant. Religion became an issue as did colour as it always did. The world had not changed.

You were sick in the car when I told you the reason they were not helpful. I didn't mean to hurt you but I wanted you to understand that it wasn't our fault. You made me stop the car and you got out. You didn't say anything to me as you left. I called but you didn't answer. I didn't know what to do. I couldn't leave the car parked in the middle of the road. I saw you walk off down the road and turn a corner. I drove after you but I couldn't find you. You never told me where you went that day. I drove the car home and cleaned up the sick you had left behind and then I waited. I waited as I had done so many times before.

You rang to say that you were at your mothers'. I wanted to come and get you but you told me not to. I knew that you needed time alone so I did not insist. I knew that even if I had done it would not have made any difference. I knew you would not have come. I rang but you must have told your parents not to answer the phone. They didn't like me, I knew that from the beginning but I thought that it would be alright. I thought it wouldn't matter so long as we had each other.

III

We got married in a church because that is what you wanted. You wanted a white wedding and that is what you had. My parents refused to come because they were disgusted with me. They said I had betrayed God. I told them I loved you and I wanted to be happy. I told them that they had lived their life and now it was my turn. They didn't speak to me for three years but I told myself that it was worth it. You didn't want children then. You were still young and I agreed that we would have a fun life before the children arrived and it was fun; for the most part. You were thirty four when we married.

When you tired of having fun I suggested that we should have children. You told me the doctors had told you that we should wait. You wouldn't tell me what the problem was and I didn't force the issue. You were the one I want-ed. I knew from the very first moment I saw you that you were the one I wanted and everything that had gone before was only to prepare me for you.

We continued to have fun though it wasn't the same. The holidays were nice. I started drinking. We got drunk together. We lived as if our lives would come to an end if we had children. It was only after your thirty-seventh birthday that I told you that the clock was ticking. That was the first time you left me. It was five days before you returned. I was wild with worry. I rang your parents and they shouted at me for not looking after you.

I told the police that you were missing. They said it was a domestic problem and they only dealt with criminal matters. I rang your work and they told me that you had taken time off and said that they didn't know where you were.

I couldn't ring my parents. They would have laughed at their only child having been so stupid to have married a white girl. I didn't have any friends. You said that you didn't like them. You told me that I could meet them without you but I didn't want to. I wanted to meet them with you. You said you loved me and that was alright. That was enough, I didn't need anything else.

When you came back you told me not to say anything. You said that you wanted to make love. We did. It was good. I didn't ask again because I didn't want to lose you. It was alright for a while after that.

IV

Donald was a surprise, a wonderful surprise. It was the best nine months of my life. I loved every minute of it even though you found it hard. He started moving at six months so that you couldn't sleep. You said it was me and moved me to the spare room. I didn't like that but that is what you wanted and I didn't want you to get upset. It wouldn't have been good for Donald.

We didn't make love but I didn't mind. You seemed to have enough worries about the birth and I loved you too much to make it harder for you. That is what love is about isn't it, caring about someone means not being selfish? I wondered why the thought of being pregnant didn't make you happy. You had worried about having a child for so long I thought you would have a wonderful time but you didn't.

The birth was difficult. They suggested not waiting. It was hard. They wanted my consent. I didn't want to risk anything happening to you or Donald. I talked to you about it but you said that it wasn't my decision and you didn't need me to decide about your baby. I know I shouldn't have but I got really mad about that. I said that it was mine as well and I had a right to share in the decision. I said that you should not be so selfish, that you should think about Donald.

You screamed at me. You told me it wasn't mine. I cried.

V

I was too hurt to forgive you but you said that you were helpless. You said that you needed me and you asked me to forgive you. You told me that you did it for us. You said you knew how much I wanted a child. You said you knew how much it hurt that I could not give you children and we couldn't afford artificial insemination. You thought that I would never find out and everything would be alright. You said that you had never loved anyone as much as you loved me. You said that you needed me and you really hoped that I could forgive you. I was glad that you loved me.

I decided that I would prove I loved you too. I forgave you and said that I would never mention anything about Donald not being mine to anyone.

I was happy when I came home. I took my colleagues out for a drink and got totally plastered. You found me in the hallway the next morning. I felt like shit but happy too. I was a husband; I had a wife and a son. I had something to live for. I worked hard and loved coming home.

You developed a terrible post natal depression. I looked after Donald for most of the early months. You refused to breast feed him. It lasted for almost a year. I told myself to be patient. I spoke to our doctor and he said that it would pass.

You came back to Donald gradually. I think it was after he had started walking.

You were jealous when he said 'da da'. You taught him to say 'ma ma'. It was funny seeing how excited you were when you got him to say 'ma ma'. You always made me smile when you behaved like a child. I don't know why I found it endearing. I suppose that is why I fell in love with you. You needed someone to look after you and I enjoyed doing that. It's a pity I didn't know you when you were at university. We were at the same university and at the same time but I didn't know you then. If we had met you wouldn't have had those awful affairs that I was sure had made you behave the way you did. You were cruel sometimes for what seemed to me to be no reason. You would hurt me as a child and I would forgive you as a parent. I wanted to make your pain go away. I loved you. I love you. Through all the tears I love you.

VI

It was two years before we knew Donald would always have a limp. For two years we thought he was just unsteady on his feet. I told you it didn't matter. I told you everything would be alright. You stopped waking up for him. I was hurt. He was our baby and you were his mother. I know he was hurt too.

I know I shouldn't have hit you but you had no right to hit Donald. It wasn't his fault. He didn't mean to break the 'Lalique' that your grandmother had left you. It was only a statuette and it was glass! You should have placed it out of his reach. He was bruised. You shouldn't have hit him so hard. I told you that you had no right to hit him. You started shouting at me. You weren't listening to me. You wouldn't accept that it was your fault. I didn't hit you hard. It was only one slap.

You left. I was annoyed too. I knew you would come back. You had to because you had left Donald behind. I laughed at how stupid you were; taking a suitcase of clothes but forgetting your own son. I didn't stop you. I was too angry.

The anger didn't last. In fact the next evening I rang your mother but you wouldn't speak to me. I couldn't take time off work so I took Donald to my sister. I asked her to look after him and she agreed. And then you rang me. You told me that you weren't coming home.

I couldn't believe the divorce. You didn't ask for custody. We sold the house and we settled financially. I was alright because I had Donald. He was more than anything money could buy. He was mine; all mine and I loved him. He loved me too.

VII

I asked my sister to tell you of the funeral. I couldn't. You didn't come. I didn't care because he was my baby not yours. I wished you had died instead of him. I hated you for not being a mother to him. He needed a mother. He needed more than I could give him.

VIII

It is funny how I survived his death. I had become numb. I thought there was nothing that would ever hurt me again. I thought that I would live my life without ever being hurt again. After all, what else could come close to losing my baby?

IX

I had almost forgotten you. Two years is a long time and then you rang. I recognised your voice.

'Hi darling, it's me.'

I didn't know what to say.

'Sweetheart, it's me. Darling, please say something. I am sorry. I love you.'

I cried. I cried for everything that day; for Donald, for my parents, for the pain that you gave me, for everything that I had felt for you and still more than all those things I cried for myself. My world ended that day. The day you said you cared. I wanted to hold you and cry all the tears that I had stored up for all those years waiting for you to show me you cared.

They said I was screaming but I didn't hear anything. All I could hear was silence. I remember crying because I remember feeling the tears on my face. They said that I was holding a telephone and I would not let go. They said that there wasn't anyone on the other end of the phone. The neighbours called an ambulance. I think I remember seeing them although everything is a blur.

X

The doctors say I will be alright if I take the medication. My office has been great. They let me come back to work and let me take time off when I can't cope. My sister comes to see me when she can. I don't go to the cemetery any more. I don't need to. My parents are looking after Donald.

*　　　*　　　*

Going out

I was surprised when John called out of the blue and asked me to meet him in town. It must have been over fifteen years since I had done that. It was still late opening in Oxford Street on Thursday night; a tradition that I thought had died ever since we had stopped going out together. Married life had taken over early in our relationship and having children early had reinforced the routine. We had our evenings when the children were not demanding but otherwise it was slumping in front of the television and the strained effort of getting out of the armchair to go to bed. Sex was usually an after thought when the dim memories of passion that one recalled revealed themselves for an all too short a diversion between lying down and falling asleep.

I laughed at the suggestion. I am not sure why I did that. I wasn't sure why John hadn't mentioned it the night before.

'Hi, Anne. What are you up to this evening? Wondered whether you would like to meet up after work. I could finish early and we could go up to Oxford Street as we used to.'

'Are you asking me out?' I laughed, 'Yes sure. I think it would be fun. Not sure what I want though.'

That was settled. I didn't need to worry about the children. Pam was fifteen and always busy in her room. It was a mistake to agree that she could have an internet connection in her bedroom and Amy, at twelve, didn't need much looking after.

Both were surprised when I broke the news to them, especially Amy who had immediately asked to come along and then looked confused as to why she couldn't. I remember thinking afterwards whether I had a similar view of my parents. Not believing they had a life beyond looking after us. I couldn't remember.

I left the house soon after the children had got back

from school and after an uneventful journey was at the main entrance of Selfridges by five o'clock. John was late as usual, a habit he had not broken in all the years that I had known him. I used to be annoyed at first and somehow just got used to it. He was always profusely apologetic and waited for me to tell him off as if he were back at school and had been caught not having done his homework. I suppose it was because he never took my inconvenience for granted that it stopped annoying me. This time he was twenty minutes late.

I passed the time not waiting for him but looking at the shoppers that I hadn't seen for such a long time. Apart from the way they dressed I wasn't sure they had changed. Late summer still had its' fair share of tourists and shoppers all of whom either hurried carrying shopping bags full of things advertised by the designer paper bags or looked through shop windows seeming to make a mental note of what they would buy on their next trip or next relationship.

'Oh I am so sorry, Anne. I had an urgent report to get out which I only got at the last moment and to top it all the Tube was delayed.'

Another boring excuse I thought to myself and ignored the rest of the explanation.

'Shall we have a look in Selfridges,' I said. 'I saw an overcoat in the shop window. Strange they should be showing off their autumn collection so early but I wanted to have a look.'

Actually I had wanted a nice overcoat for my fortieth birthday last year but John had absentmindedly forgotten all my hints and had bought me a picture instead. It was a nice picture and now I had three by the same artist but I would have liked a coat. It is not that I couldn't buy one myself. We had, after all, long forgotten monthly budgets to make ends meet thanks to success at work but somehow it was always nicer when John bought me something.

We found the department and seeing the coats John

moved into the background. I don't know whether this is a purely female trait but I have for some time been conscious of losing John in supermarkets or shopping centres when I had something to look at or buy. John would walk around for hours trying to find me although now in the days of mobile telephones life is a lot easier.

I looked through the overcoats feeling the material as I went along the rail. Wool, wool and cashmere mix, cashmere, mohair. Strange tingling sensations as I felt the price of the overcoats get higher. I turned to make sure John was still there and had not walked off. He was.

'What do you think John? Is there something that you like?'

'Well,' he said trying to look interested, 'they all look nice, umm, the darker colours suit you.'

That was a good recovery. I smiled in encouragement.

'Why don't you try one of them on?'

The mohair felt wonderful. I didn't look at the price on purpose. That would have spoilt it. I looked for my size. It used to be a 10 but now a 14 that I was no longer ashamed of. John helped me on with the coat. For a moment I forgot that I was forty-one years old and our relationship was unconsciously familiar and did a swirl.

John smiled. For a split second we were in love again and I was nineteen. It felt wonderful and I was determined to make the feeling last for as long as I could. John, being forty-four years old, broke the spell.

'How much is it?'

I put it back in its rack with a little unnoticeable sigh.

I strolled through the other departments still smarting at the rude awakening and it was only when we got to the perfumery that I sensed a return to the mischievousness that I had delighted in with the overcoats. I purposely slowed my step through the perfumery. John turned to understand why I had changed my pace, checked his own and for a moment looked perplexed. I smiled reassuringly and he was back to his unsuspecting self. I enjoyed sensing John's pupils dilate at the over made up sales assistants who smelled as if body odour had turned into expensive perfumes in the magical land of promise. I had, in the early days of inexperience, once caught John looking a little longer that he could get away with and used that to exact revenge when he found fault with me meeting him in bed fully made up. I had long since learned that men have an innate desire to make the call and all they allow us is either to be the whore if they permitted or if necessity required it to function out of habit. In the early days it always made me indignant to think that John could be excited by how other women dressed but would not allow me to excite him by dressing as they did but then, that was a long time ago.

John looked. I thought it funny at first and then something inside me snapped and caused me to pick up my pace and almost storm out of the department.

'Everything alright, Anne?'

I took a deep breath. It was silly to get annoyed with John if it was going to give me the impossible task of trying to explain my feelings.

'It's alright, dear. I think it was just a little too crowded in there. A little fresh air and I will be fine.'

We walked along. This time I took John's arm even though walking two abreast in Oxford Street on a late opening night is not easy. I remembered how we had done this a long time ago, looking for some shoes. I had enjoyed myself then and wondered whether it would be as much fun as it had been.

'Do you remember, John? Those red shoes that we got for your first office Christmas party after we got married.'

John struggled. I could see his mind shifting through memories that had been filed a long time ago. I pushed ahead hoping the encouragement might speed things up.

'Will you buy me some shoes today?'

'Yes of course darling. I remember the red shoes. Cost a fortune! What ever happened to them?'

Our memories were not the same. It wasn't the red shoes I wanted to remember.

We walked along. The air became a quietly cool and the grey overcast sky threatened a drizzle as if we had just entered the pages of a novel by Hardy. I didn't want to look at shoes anymore and wondered what on earth we were doing. I thought about what the children might be up to. Pam would probably be on the internet and Amy would be watching television, probably a serial that gave her the feeling of being grown up. I used to watch her as she looked through a kissing scene as if it was something that she was used to and did not need to be embarrassed by them any more. My mind came back to the crowds of people we walked passed. We were a married couple to whom conversation had become a communication tool and no longer the adventure that it once must have been.

The silence was awkward only because we were not in the familiar environment of home where distractions are always plentiful. I turned to John as we crossed the street just checking that he was still with me. He too turned and smiled. The years had been kind to him. His full head of greying hair made him looked distinguished. I suddenly felt proud of him and took his arm. He gave me another smile and patted my hand.

'What are we going to do?' I asked. It was getting boring walking around with no purpose. Years of doing things because they had to be done had programmed me into feeling uncomfortable not having to do anything. Even when we went on those rare beach holidays the children always kept me busy while John read the paper or one of those interminable best sellers that the train journey to work had introduced him to.

'I thought you wanted to buy some red shoes.'

'No darling, that was a joke.'

John looked puzzled. It was clear that he didn't understand the joke and waited to see if I was going to explain it to him. I didn't feel like it. In fact I didn't really know how I would be able to explain it anyway.

'What would you like to do darling?'

I had hoped that he would decide something. After all it

was John who had asked me out. It was the same as all those years ago. I remember our very first date was a call asking me whether I was doing anything after work and whether I would like to meet up. We had met in a bar and I waited all evening for the suggestion of something else promised for the evening. Even something quite predictable such as a film or dinner or both but nothing happened. John, obviously getting hungry, praised the bar for its cuisine and we ended up eating there.

'Are you hungry?' I asked, while at the same time wondering where we could eat if John said he was. John was bound to ask me to decide.

John replied as expected and I wondered whether a tearoom that we had visited all those years ago still existed. John didn't know but we decided to set off in search of it even though it was way past teatime and we would be spoiling dinner.

The search for the tearooms sparked off an adventure that the evening was beginning to need with desperation and I was glad of it, even more so when not being able to remember the name of the road we still managed to find it. It was new in those days and very fashionable to have something that was such a tradition in the middle of London. A little dowdy now which gave the impression of no change in ownership over the years but still it brought back memories of a once romantic journey to matrimony that we enjoyed mapping out together. We found a table immediately and our waitress, an Australian student I suspect, handed us our menus and took our order with an air of efficiency that seemed a little out of place in the tradition of an English tea-house. I saw John notice the shortness of her very un-Victorian skirt as she walked away but didn't think embarrassing him was appropriate.

'Strange uniform.'

'Yes.'

The scones and jams arrived with toast and tea and we ate with no worry about heart disease, cholesterol or waistlines. Our conversation punctured our enjoyment of the delights of decadence with 'Mmms' and 'Good, isn't it' until bloated with sugar and awash with tea we sat there satisfied in a guilt free environment looking for a subject to start the communication that is a requirement of two people sitting opposite each other.

'Have you had a nice time?' asked John.

'Yes darling. It was lovely. We should do this more often.' I squeezed his hand with affection but then overcome with the unusual tenderness of the evening I added, 'I love you John, I love you very much.'

We got home late. Amy was already asleep and Pam was lying in bed watching the television that had cost three years of tantrums.

I had a shower and John waited for me in bed. We could hear Pam's television so made love quietly. It was nice to feel special again. It is always nice to feel special and I can never understand why we don't feel like that more often.

The children have left home and John retired last year. I don't remember being asked out since that lovely evening although we have been all over the world together. I wonder whether the tearoom is still there and who is buying red shoes now.

*　　　*　　　*

Black & White

I

Debating what is right or wrong in life is a pastime for most human beings. For some this takes the more active form of protest marches, violence on the streets or other demonstration of a commitment to change but for most of us it provides a basis of social interaction. We meet friends who come from the same socio-economic background and therefore equipped with a similar education to allow neither to patronise the other that would otherwise disrupt the agreeable passing of time.

It was at a dinner party that I first met Simon. He was then in his early forties, divorced, well read and most of all opinionated. I was in a town not far away on business and had not seen Judy and Mike ever since they had decided to move out of London some four years earlier. They had been good friends while in London and we made it a point of meeting up at least for a drink every few weeks. I liked them both. Judy and I had worked together until maternity leave that coincided with Mike's success gave her the inspiration of giving up her career to become a happy housewife. Although unfashionable in terms of what was then the consensus on gender politics she defended her decision with a shrug of the shoulders that annoyed any feminists she encountered and irritated husbands who relied on the financial contribution of their wives.

I had telephoned as soon as I knew that I would be in the vicinity and Mike insisted that I should plan to spend the weekend with them. Having finished work late on the Friday I decided to have a good nights rest and then catch the train up to see them. Judy had come to pick me up from the station having left the two children at home with Mike. She said she had used the excuse to have a little break and at the same time to make sure that Mike didn't forget that they were his children too. It was on the way home that she told me that they were having a dinner party that evening and had invited some of Mike's colleagues with their wives. She was sure I would enjoy the party although she was still having some difficulty in making up the even numbers she needed. Judy was meticulous about things like that. I called her a snob for her pretensions in the egalitarian society in which we lived and she always retorted that my socialist pretensions were twenty years out of date. Both statements were true in part but neither of us was prepared to change the convictions formed during our university days and that luck had allowed us the privilege of keeping. The best part of it was that we met as if the four years had been four weeks. The passage of time had allowed the children to enter what she described as the 'difficult teens' and Judy to grey a little but nothing else had changed.

They had a nice house that didn't fit the 'moving out of London-type house' I had imagined. Backing onto a golf course it was a comfortable four bed roomed semi-detached house in a pretty tree lined street. It was clear seeing the house that the privilege of living on one income had its downside. One had to make do with a little less than one would otherwise have been able to explain away but Judy seemed to be happy to accept the quiet domesticity of lower middle class living and I admired her for that.

I understood what looking after teenage children meant when Judy let me into the house to find Mike having fallen asleep in front of the television with the children in their bedrooms amusing themselves.

We spent an agreeable day drinking beers and catching up on old times. I had never spent so much time with Mike before but found him easy to get along with. I could see what Judy saw in him. The children were old enough to create a hushed silence in the house; each in their own bedroom carefully keeping their lives secret from interfering parents. Both were going over to stay with friends that evening which meant that they would not be around for the dinner party.

After lunch Judy decided that we had relaxed for long enough and got us both working on salads. Mike complained as husbands are allowed to and I enthused as I was expected to.

II

Dinner was set at seven-thirty for eight and by seven forty-five everyone was there except Simon. I found it a little odd that Judy had not found a female partner for me but then this was not a formal dinner party and I was somewhat relieved by the prospect of not having to deal with a blind date.

Simon was a little late but we spent the time usefully nursing pre-dinner drinks. The twelve for dinner were seated with Simon and myself at opposite ends of the table, which as the conversation at dinner progressed, was the best thing to do.

It was a friendly group who knew each other well. Simon was a new member of the group with a different view of the world that I suspected came with the selfishness of only having himself to think about. It was not until coffee was served that he decided to make a contribution. A comment from by Mike inspired Simon to speak.

'You know I cannot understand why we have to get involved in world affairs when we have enough problems at home.'

It was an innocent enough remark but Simon took it seriously. The fact that his voice had not been heard before made everyone stop what they were doing and turn their attention to him.

'If something is wrong we need to stand up and say what we think.'

It was a bold statement, more said in the vein of a party political speech than a response at dinner.

'I am sorry to disagree Simon, but do you really think we have the right to interfere in the politics of another country. After all we wouldn't take it very kindly if some

26

foreigner did that to us.'

'It depends who says it and if they were right then we should accept the criticism.'

'That is a noble stand but I do not think you would do that if it actually happened.'

He smiled, I thought condescendingly.

'I am not a pacifist,' he said, 'I believe in standing up for what I believe is right.'

'But how can you be sure that you are in the right? Isn't that a matter of opinion?'

'No, what is right is right and is obvious. I do not think one can have a different opinion about what is evidently 'right'.'

We covered Iraq, Iran and the United States, women's rights, freedom to express one's sexuality, capitalism, communism and freedom of speech. There were some other minor topics which I do not now recall but what I remember is whatever was discussed his answer was clear, unambiguous and confident. I was struck by his inflexibility and more so by the fact that looking back I did not find his certainty irritating. In fact, quite the opposite, I envied his breadth of knowledge about all the topics we discussed. He never argued, merely stating his opinion with the knowledge that none could convince him otherwise. The others at the table enjoyed the banter offering remarks that fuelled the discussion.

It was Judy that finally cracked under the pressure. Her irritation was surprising as she was the hostess and therefore was the last person permitted by the rules of a dinner party to 'put down' a guest. I suspect the wine had something to do with it.

'So Simon, when are you getting married again?'

Simon was taken aback by the question. Everyone noticed the extra few seconds he needed to formulate a response.

Simon had been divorced for about four years. It had been an ugly divorce. The reasons officially cited for the divorce were 'irreconcilable differences'.

'I don't think I am ready for marriage again. Once is enough.'

Mike, much to the obvious irritation of Judy, joked about the free life of the bachelor.

'No Mike, there is nothing wonderful about life free from responsibility. It is fun for a while but then it becomes more meaningless than the boredom of marriage.'

'Are you becoming a monk?'

'No, Judy, I am just saying that I don't think I am ready to try it again. I had the best possible opportunity to make a go of it but failed. I still don't know why but it did. The shock of divorce without betrayal as a cause is the most painful. I had the feeling that I was the luckiest man in the world and that scared me even when we were together. The feeling of impending doom but then Lisa laughed off my fears. I fought hard to get her to say why the marriage had come to an end and God knows it cost me ten times more in legal fees than it needed to without a result. Those solicitors know how to make money!'

For some reason the change in conversation made me feel sad.

'Lay off Judy, leave the poor man alone.'

'No, he thinks he is a 'know it all', has an opinion on every subject under the sun but when it comes down to it he hasn't got answers to the basic one of how to keep a relationship going.'

Mike thankfully intervened. Judy had gone too far. It was an awkward end to the dinner party. Simon was the first to leave.

III

I got Simon's phone number from John a few weeks later and that is how we became friends.

Simon is still as opinionated as he was the first time I met him and he is still single. I have met a few of his girl-friends some of whom have been very nice and some I know who have wanted something more permanent. Whenever

I have asked Simon why he doesn't take a chance his reply is always the same, 'I'm not sure.'

*   *   *

Coming out of the dream

I

It was like coming out of a dream. I never expected that the realisation would come with such a gentle sigh. I thought it would be a 'kicking and screaming' thing, more like childbirth than what it turned out to be. As always the joke is that it always comes too late.

Mine was a good life. I had a job that I didn't like but passed the time lucratively. My wife and I had stopped making love long enough ago to wonder what it had been like and whether it had really happened despite the existence of two children that called us Mummy and Daddy. Of course the children no longer needed me except to accuse me of giving them an environment that they couldn't wait to get out of especially as they had grown up enough not to care whether I was angry with them or not. My friends were all fair weather friends which meant that they were never there when I needed them and relatives were the usual pain that comedians portrayed so very well at deaths, marriages and Christmas; apologetic for long absences, surprise at finally having made the commitment and of course bitter for having to make the forced reunion when it would have been more pleasurable to have watched the Queens Speech followed by Lawrence of Arabia.

It wasn't a bad life. I enjoyed the routine of it all. Fast cars, getting drunk on Fridays and the continuous mode of illicit affairs at the office spiced up with gossip about closet lesbians and homosexuals never held much attraction for me. I enjoyed the pleasure of searching for nothing in particular and wanting even less.

I do not want you to think that I was in any way miserable. I was indeed happy with my lot and the reason was simple. I knew there was nothing better out there. Memories are flawed and one never remembered enough of the good times to make it worthwhile accumulating any more. Forty years of doing that was more than enough time wasted and I had spent the last nine enjoying the comfort of eating regularly, sleeping well, not working too hard and spending my time learning to become a mediocre gardener.

II

I suppose the first indication that something was going to happen was being passed over for promotion. I didn't expect it but consoled myself. My boss knew he had passed me over, I knew the company could not afford to lose me at that particular time, which together meant that he would need to pay blood money. The affected temporary friendliness and a pay rise were, I felt, adequate compensation. I knew the routine. It had been played too often for anyone to take any notice but we still obliged with exaggerated disappointment, understanding and consolation from colleagues. We all knew that there was the Company and then there was Us, each screwing the other with the semblance of civility and outwardly good intention. We all knew that colleagues were secretly pleased that one of their number was suffering and not them.

My wife was understanding, the children didn't indicate they had noticed and if they did I am sure that secretly they expected no better from their loser of a father. Friends exclaimed what a shame it was in between discussions about politics, sport or sex.

The second indication came with Sally staying out late. She was sixteen and while she had permission to see a film with her friends in between revising for GCSEs her mother assured me that it did not extend to the smell of a cheap wine even if she was still in possession of all of her faculties. A talkative child with opinions on every subject as most young people, Sally was the darling of the family. Our first child that had taken the time to teach us to be better parents was now testing her ability to flee the nest. It would take her at least another three years before she would be able to assert any independence that could be taken seriously and in that knowledge the challenge was met with a firm hand.

The reaction was unexpected. My wife, the instigator of the reprimand, fled at the first sight of blood. Well actually it was Sally screaming at me for daring to tell her not to shout at her mother that caused the retreat. The loneliness of a father confronted with a daughter who refused to listen to him left me tongue-tied and shaking. Standing there in the middle of an empty living room with doors being slammed all around me was not an ideal situation.

I resigned myself to the fate of middle-aged men, sat down in my favourite armchair and switched on the television. I had done it before and it seemed to do the trick. My wife would come in after an hour or so to tell me dinner was ready or, if we had eaten, whether I would like a cup of tea. It was tea I waited for this time.

Despite what may seem obvious to you I only speculate in hindsight as to when it should have become obvious that something was about to happen.

III

I saw John walking his dog in the park. He was a neighbour four houses along that I saw for a number of years catch the same train to work. He had retired with his old dog that no longer appreciated the extra attention now being given to him. His wife died a year ago and I went to the funeral. My wife didn't want to come. He let a tear fall at the service, which was a nice touch. There were not many people there and I remember wondering how many people would be at my funeral. Disappointed at the number I came up with I decided I did not want a funeral. The trouble was when you have a family it is difficult to avoid one. Even soldiers blown to bits in some far off war had a funeral. I wondered whether I would be contacted when John died so that I could attend his funeral.

'Hello John, do accept my deepest condolences.'

I wanted to say sincerest but thought that would sound

insincere. I didn't really know his wife. In fact I had only found out about the funeral through some idle chat with my immediate neighbour who mentioned that John had lost his wife and asked whether I wanted to come along to the funeral. I didn't really want to but then thought it might be better than going in to work. We got special time off from work for bereavement.

'Thank you, good of you to come.'

He didn't mention my name once and I was sure that he had forgotten it. I didn't mind. I enjoyed the funeral and the service. They sang an old school favourite hymn despite it sounding different with only eight people. I was surprised that John had bothered with a hymn.

I didn't say much when I got home. I actually felt sad.

John had aged since the death of his wife. It did cross my mind to wonder how lonely he actually felt but then I knew it must feel lonely without the comfort of having someone around. Having spent all ones life balancing the demands of others on your time and then when you had all the time in the world you find yourself left on your own.

It was the funeral that made me recall the dream.

IV

I met a girl who was nice. I hesitated in making the intro-duction and was delighted with the result. We had found each other and fallen in love. We got married and had two beautiful children that were absolutely no bother at all. We brought them up without experiencing any crises that others we knew must go through. Our children grew up to become our pride and joy. The girl I married aged with grace and when the children left home we spent our time in the comfort of pleasant memories. When she died I lost the will to live and followed her into the next world as soon as I could. We are happy together.

I cried.

V

The cancer was not diagnosed until it was too late. I died six weeks later. My wife has sorted out the probate, the children are back in their routine and I am well. I am gently coming out of the dream.

*   *   *

Fragments

I

I saw you walk down the street. I was there in the office when you left, rushed to the balcony and searched frantically. I didn't know which street you would walk down so I paced up and down to either end until I saw you leave the building. You had a large bag on your shoulder and a small case in which I imagined you had taken your computer home with you to do some work. Why didn't you stay in the office? Why couldn't you have spent the evening here. You wouldn't have noticed me. I would have been extremely careful so as not to let on that I was interested. I don't know why I was interested but I was. I just was. You could have worked away and I would not have bothered you.

As you walked down the street, your form becoming smaller as the distance grew between us, I wondered whether you would turn to look back. If you did what would I do? I had no idea. If I smiled as you noticed me would you have seen my smile? Would you have seen the pleading in my eyes for you to stay with me? I would have found something to work on and only walked past you to get a coffee. I would have said hello as I walked past. You would have looked up and smiled. I would have photographed that smile with all the concentration that I could conjure up to retain the image that I wanted to hold. I would have imagined you looking in the mirror but there would not have been a mirror, just me, and you would not have noticed. I would have cast a spell that would have held you transfixed on your imaginary mirror as if you had noticed a wrinkle and concentrated on willing it away.

II

I said goodbye to you. I did not want to go but I had to. I was tired. The strain of being so close was unbearable. I could smell you. Your perfume had melted into the fragrance of your body and I was pleased. It was torture to sit with you and not hold you. I sat there watching the film that played, a film that had no meaning for me. I widened the range of my vision to get close to you. I was careful. No one saw me but it strained my eyes. The film became a blur. I had seen it before but had lied to you.

Your phone rang and despite the protests of your friends I stopped the film. You told me not to bother but I knew that if I didn't precious minutes would pass by and shorten the evening. I didn't have a drink because I was on a mission. I didn't want to get caught. No one could notice because if they did then you would know and then something would have happened. I don't know what, but something would have happened. I am sure. I didn't want to hear you say that you didn't like me enough to be mine. I didn't want to take that risk. I knew that I would have to know one day but there was no point taking that chance now.

I kissed you on the cheeks. I forced myself to keep it natural so that you would not notice. I held my breath as I did so. I didn't want to be betrayed by my mind letting go of its control of my body. I said goodbye but I didn't want to go.

You smiled. I think it was an innocent smile, one that you kept for acquaintances or friends from whom you needed nothing but conversation. I saw your lips part as you smiled. Your mouth was moist, a little green speck in between your teeth, part of the salad in the sandwich that you had eaten, a speck of seaweed caught among the rocks within a receding sea of red.

Your eyes sparkled despite the tiredness that the evening had brought you. Your breath smelled of the food that you had eaten. It wasn't unpleasant. I know it would have been unpleasant if it had been mine but it wasn't. It was yours.

I saw you move in your jeans. They were not as tight a fit as you had hoped. They covered you as well as the t-shirt you wore with a cartoon character that I could not identify. I would have if you had let me look at the t-shirt without noticing me but I couldn't take that chance.

III

I waited for your call or an SMS. I checked my phone so many times and then decided the best way would be to stare at it. I didn't know what I would do if you rang. I waited for two hours but you did not ring. I gave up waiting and decided to stare at the television. I don't know what was on. It didn't matter. I lay down on the sofa and watched the same program. The remote was too far from me to make the effort to change the channel. I fell asleep on the sofa and entered a dream specially prepared for me. You were in my dream. I knew you would be because I had especially asked for you when ordering the dream. You were wearing jeans and a t-shirt. I stared at the t-shirt. I didn't care if you noticed because I knew I was having a dream. I stared at your t-shirt to make out what the cartoon character was but couldn't. I tried hard but couldn't. I ordered the dream maker to place a cartoon character that I would recognise. They agreed to do so and went off to look in the archives.

I turned to your face. You were looking at me and smiling. You knew I was looking at you but I didn't care. I could do anything I wanted. It was my dream. I turned to your t-shirt again and stared. I could see the form of your breasts but only the outline. The dream makers had not allowed anything vulgar. I didn't mind. Dreams that allowed you to be vulgar were expensive and I had not paid enough. The dream makers only allowed those dreams if you agreed to give up the right to know you were dreaming. I didn't want that. I wanted control over my dream of you.

The phone rang with the SMS message tone. It woke me from my dream. I was annoyed because it interrupted the dream that I had paid for. The dream makers were not stupid. They knew how to make money. Once you left the dream for no matter what reason they would not allow you back without another payment. I was annoyed at the interruption.

The television was still switched on and playing the same program. I was annoyed. I decided to make the television pay for the interruption. I got up to change the channel. The remote control lay by my phone. The pulsating light of the phone made the phone feel alive. I picked it up and stared at the screen of my phone. It showed an SMS unread. I opened the phone to scroll to the SMS menu and opened the SMS.

I smiled. My heart raced. I wanted to scream with joy. I switched it on and read your message. You asked whether I had got home alright. I knew you liked me. I knew it from the very first time our eyes met. You had to because I liked you so much. The SMS proved it.

IV

It was your voice that first attracted me to you. I noticed it the very first time I heard you speak. You weren't speaking to me but that didn't matter. I turned around and there you were. You were speaking to a colleague at a work station next to me. You looked up and said hello. That hello was mine. It chimed one tone lower than the rest. It was like hearing the sound of a minor note when there were only major notes playing all around me. It wasn't out of place in the music of the conversation around me but noticeable because it was special. It echoed through my mind all afternoon. It was only when I went home that I couldn't hear your voice. I think it was because you were too far from me. I think sound also has a limit in terms of how far it can travel in the world of memory.

I wanted to talk to you that day but I didn't know what to

talk about. I didn't want to say something stupid because I knew I would only have one chance, only one chance to engage in conversation with you. I knew about open questions. I had read that somewhere. They were questions that allowed you to engage in long conversations. I practiced that afternoon but couldn't find one that I could be sure would do the trick.

Colleagues were going to see a film and asked me if I wanted to come along. I said I couldn't go just in case you would work late. I wondered whether I would have a chance to have a conversation with you after everyone had gone. It would be easier without witnesses to any failure that I may have.

I might ask you whether you would like to go out for a drink, or a meal, or spend the rest of your life with me, but you left early.

I raced to the balcony to see whether I could see you walking home. I didn't know which street you might take so paced up and down the balcony but I didn't see you. I worked late because I was disappointed. My boss thought I was trying to impress and I wanted him to think that I was trying to impress, it was better than him knowing the truth. My boss thinks I am stupid but he is the stupid one. I could use him to distract me from the disappointment. I said that I wanted to finish up what I had so that I could concentrate on something new in the morning. I said that I didn't like leaving things half finished. I said that I had some ideas which I needed to capture while I had them. I hoped that I would be right and give him a good piece of work the next morning. He listened and complimented me on my conscientiousness. Idiot!

He left. I didn't want to do any more but I had to because of the promise to give him something in the morning. It was hard concentrating on my work. I didn't finish until very late and I was tired. The tiredness helped ease the pain of my disappointment.

I worked late every day that week hoping that you would do the same but you didn't. You went for a drink with colleagues from another department but I found out too late to try and get invited too. It was probably better that way because I wanted you all to myself, not with others around you. I couldn't be sure that I would be able to steal glances without anyone noticing, and you know how callous people can be in those situations. It would be hard enough if we were alone.

V

I was glad that you became friends with Leanne. She was a nice girl but plain. I knew she did not have a boyfriend and I also knew that she was fishing for one. She had flirted with me on more than one occasion and I had ignored her. She was not my type. I heard her invite you to a 'film fest' on Saturday and you said yes. It was an Akiri Kurusawa night. Three films; Seven Samurai, Kagemusha and Ran. I had seen them all.

I didn't realise you liked films.

I wanted to invite you to a 'film fest' on Saturday night. If I had asked you would you have said yes? I could have got the films that you wanted to see. I have seen so many films I could have suggested something. I could have introduced you to Chinese or Korean rather than old Japanese films. Kurusawa is dead. What's the point? Why not branch out. Expand your mind!

'Hi, Leanne, how are you?' I said with a smile. One of those practiced smiles that come with the experience of countless failed attempts

'Fine, you seem happy today.'

'Oh nothing, you look good.'

'Thanks, didn't think you'd notice.'

'Hey, do you fancy going out sometime.'

'Are you asking me out on a date?'

Well I did not mean a date you stupid cow. I wanted to ask HER out and if it hadn't been for you I might have done. So now, I am trying something else. You see I am not stupid. I know how to play these games as well.

'Well, OK, a date, anything wrong with that? It's OK if you don't want to.'

'You know Roy, I would love to.'

She smiled.

'Great. How about this Saturday?'

'Oh shit! I can't this Saturday. I am having a Japanese film fest. Do you like Japanese films? Akiri Kurusawa? Can you come?'

'What are you watching? Seven Samurai, Ran or Kagemusha? That probably covers his genre.'

'You know that is amazing. Those were the three films June and I chose.'

'Good choice. I'll come.'

'We can always go out next weekend if you like, Roy'

'Yeah. Sure.'

Well, what do you think of that! I told you I was not stupid.

That week was good for me. My boss called me in and told me he was really pleased with the great job that I had been doing. I went out on Friday night to celebrate. I got totally plastered. I was happy. The hangover on Saturday morning didn't bother me. I slept until lunchtime and then got ready to come over to you. You would be there and that was all that mattered.

VI

You kissed everyone as you came in. You kissed me too, on the cheeks. You came in with John and Rachel. They made a nice couple.

I impressed you with my knowledge of Kurusawa. We talked that evening. You sat next to me on the sofa. Your hips touched mine as you squeezed in between John and me. I know you did that on purpose and I thanked you for it.

You listened to me talk of the films. You argued with me and I let you win even though I knew you were wrong. You told Leanne that I didn't know as much about films as she had said I did. Leanne defended me. I stopped her to acknowledge your victory.

They played Ran before the others. That was stupid. It was his last film and should have been played last. You didn't notice that. You didn't say anything.

Ran is a long film. There were too many people there.

Leanne was upset that I left early. I said something about having promised a friend I would go and see him. They stopped the film. Everyone seemed disappointed and despite the protests I left.

VII

I rang you back. I wanted to hear your voice. An SMS would not have been enough. The words had to be said with your lips, and your smile, and your fragrance and your whole being. I would have all that in your voice.

'Hi, thanks for the SMS.'

'That's all right. We just wanted to know whether you got home alright. Leanne's phone is dead. She was worried. Here, I'll pass the phone over.'

'Hello, Roy, are you alright.'

*   *   *

Emma

I

It was a long time coming but the visit had finally been organized and the expected day marked in a diary that had long been a record of disappointments. Emma lay in bed lazily staring at the ceiling as only a life of living alone would allow. There was no one to bother her, no one to get up for and no one but herself to worry about. The thirty six years that she had spent on this lonely planet had given her plenty of time to indulge herself with relationships born of puberty and teenage rebellion, adolescent independence, university freedom, adult desperation and boredom. She often looked back at her life with some regret. Each period had started with such excitement and somehow without any warning had inspired a dramatic change of direction. It was like a conversation that one had difficulty in remembering how the topic of discussion had been selected and yet had the same desperation of continuing to try and remember even though one knew from experience that it would be futile.

Steven belonged to the past. Introduced at university their relationship had continued through adulterous affairs and now after a gap of six years a phone call had broken the silence. Emma smiled at the thought that throughout all that had happened she had still kept the house that she had wisely bought within six months of leaving university. Her father had offered to help when she had decided to allow Brian to move in with her and Emma, in one of those rare moments of magnanimity on her part, had allowed him to help. She had not been greedy. All she had accepted was half the deposit and a guarantee for the mortgage. Brian didn't last long. An affair with Steven had made her realize that it wasn't fun living a lie and coupled with the outside chance that Steven would ask her to move in with him made her tell Brian the truth. It was the first time she had ever seen anyone cry over losing her and she, in sympathy, cried an apology as she left the restaurant in which the scene had been acted with dramatic effect.

Steven was going through a divorce and needed a shoulder to cry on. That was the gist of the telephone call although Emma knew that was code to allow him back again for the comfort of free sex and a place to stay. It was going to be her choice. Emma was not fool enough to believe that Steven was calling for the comfort of a platonic friendship.

Steven had asked whether he could come over to see her after work one evening and suggested Friday so that they would not have to worry about work the next day but Emma was not that gullible. She wanted the option of saying no so picked Thursday evening after work at a restaurant equidistant from where they both lived.

Emma had been relatively celibate for the last two years indulging in infrequent drunken one night stands that were best left unremembered. The meeting with Steven, however, rekindled a once girlish hope of permanence. Independent living had been easy once she had realized that she need not dwell on the past. She had trained her memory to be selective. Nothing uncomfortable was allowed to intrude. The failures of the past were put down to experience with promises not to allow them to be repeated and even when they were it was easy to persuade herself that they were not repetitions. Emma had decided to put every mistake into a new file marked 'New experience – worth having had but not worth repeating' so that she could avoid the anti-depressants that friends would prescribe from time to time.

Steven had let her down the first time. All the other times she, Emma, had made the decisions. He had hurt her once and ever since then she had allowed him to meet her if she wanted to, slept with him when she wanted and left him when she had wanted to. It was a better way of living. If she had thought about it long enough she would have realized that no-one is able to get away with that kind of living. She was attractive enough for someone to proposition her whenever she was feeling down and experienced enough to make sure that the pleasure was not all one sided so that whenever the ending of the relationship threatened to disrupt her world she was able to get through without having to go to pieces. Brian was the exception. He was nice but then again relationships rarely survive because couples are nice to each other. Steven had provided the passion missing in the relationship and Emma had taken the risk of losing what she had because she had thought the risk worth taking. The disappointment was not as badly felt as she had thought but she acted the role of regret for the comfort of friends and family.

'Well Steven, what have you got to offer me this time, you bastard? If nothing else I hope you are going to be good in bed!'

II

He looked very much the same as she had imagined he would. A little older but age had not encouraged much more than affected courtesy. He obviously felt that he would have to try harder and Emma played on his anxiety. Men were strange, always trying hard when they didn't need to.

The dinner was a dull affair. The pasta was plain and the wine not drinkable. Steven complimented her on her looks and with the subtlety of a teenager hinted at the possibility of regret for missed opportunities that he imagined they had had. Thinking that her sympathy would be gained by the break up of his marriage he laboured in boring detail of all things that were wrong. Emma tried to distract him from his self indulgence by excusing herself twice to visit the ladies room pondering each time whether she had let him try hard enough but then decided to let him work a little longer. She knew what he wanted and had tidied up her flat for the occasion.

'Emm, I know I have no right to ask but could I come over?'

It was corny. Something broke. All the planning seemed to go out of the window. Emma was surprised that she was happy to delay the moment that she had spent the best part of the day planning for.

'Steven, I don't thing anything is going to happen tonight, wrong time of the month. I agreed to come because I thought you just wanted to talk.'

Amused at seeing him go on the defensive she was happy to apologise for misunderstanding him.

The date ended shortly after the exchange. Steve drove her home and left with the promise to let him call again.

It was almost midnight by the time she got home and so after a short dose of late night television tucked into the crisp new sheets that held no risk of disappointment. She was finally over Steven.

*   *   *

Joan

'You know I really didn't want to fly today, I really didn't.'

Joan was upset at having to leave a day earlier than she had intended. She had fallen in love with the city ever since she had braved her first holiday after her husband had died nine years ago. She had tried to find a landlady that would be happy to put her up each year but somehow something always went wrong. They would agree to check with each other on each departure but every time except the first she had been unable to secure the room for the period she wanted.

The flight was a short one. Three and half hours of frantic service by the air crew that watered, fed, cleared away and still managed to get in a selling spree with duty free goods that somehow always found customers despite a choice that would not otherwise have satisfied a corner shop customer.

There were many beautiful cities in the world to choose from and sitting one day shortly after the fourth anniversary of her husbands death in her flat in Eaton Place she decided to pick one that offered her a city unknown to her in which a language was spoken that bore no resemblance to any language Joan knew. St Petersburg, a city in Russia with a pretence of being seen as completely European was the one she picked. The choice was not one that was borne of any logical thought process or excited desire for adventure but one simply because the brochure offered her a package tour that was within the small pension a late marriage and early death of her husband offered her.

The address may sound elegant but the reality was that this was a small flat in nowhere as grand a place as Eaton Square and even for the address was a small studio flat on the top floor in the least salubrious part of the building. Not that she complained. She had been a happy thirty eight year old unmarried secretary living on her own in a small flat left to her by her mother. The house in Putney her husband had left her was let and provided her with an income that allowed her to buy presents for nephews and nieces thus guaranteeing invitations that otherwise would have been pot luck.

She had enjoyed the first trip so much that she had filled her flat with a variety of souvenirs that looked completely out of place among the few pieces of English furniture that various uncles and aunts had left her. But she liked them. It was her private life, not the lonely life she had looking after an invalid mother or learning about the joys of marriage with a husband who believed that a wife in England was worth having after many years as an expatriate where the comforts of life came with the job.

It had been hard finding a job after her husband died. Somehow in the days of computers not many had any use for shorthand or speed typing although perhaps it was also partly that it was not easy to compete with the younger more eager job hunters.

Joan hadn't wanted to give up her job and it had never occurred to her that she would have to when she agreed to get married. Harry, her husband, was one of those men who expected things to happen as he imagined they should and would be at a complete loss when challenged. 'Are you serious Joan? I can't believe you just said that. You better go and lie down. You are obviously having a bad day.' And that would be the end of that.

Russia or more correctly the fall of the Soviet Union had given her a wonderful lease of life. He husband was excited by it and never stopped talking about it. Joan listened and learned which helped her develop a fascination that gave her a purpose. She never again had to hear her husband complain about the lack of imagination she showed in her selection of birthday or Christmas presents. Anything connected with the former Soviet Union was gleefully accepted with warmth that often embarrassed her. Four years she had of this before her husband died. She had been taken by surprise. At fifty-eight years old she thought he still had a good few years in him. She had always hoped that it would not be a long and tortuous illness that would be the prelude to a death that one waited for and ultimately hoped for but the heart attack was sudden. Without warning, one Sunday afternoon while she was putting the Sunday lunch dishes away Harry had keeled over and never regained consciousness. It had taken her a few minutes to decide to call for an ambulance and had even been apologetic to the emergency services operator for disturbing their Sunday. She had been upset by the death but had held her dignity throughout the funeral and had not once shed a tear in public. The short marriage ended with a performance that she knew her husband would have wanted.

'I really didn't want to leave but I had to. My visa expired tomorrow but I could only get onto the waiting list for tomorrow's flight. I really wasn't ready to travel. I didn't sleep all night. My landlady was worried about me taking a chance. She said that I would have a problem at the airport and she would get into trouble. I was third on the waiting list and British Airways said that I would probably be alright.'

Joan was unhappy. So self absorbed in her unhappiness that she seemed to ignore the glazed look of her fellow passenger who had shortly after their first exchange lost interest.

The fifth of her visits to the 'Venice of the north' had not been a success. The weather as far as her memory could tell had been unusual in that it had rained almost every September day. The residents had not been as kind as they had been in the earlier trips despite Joan making a concerted effort to practice the Russian she had spent the last two years at evening classes mastering. She knew her accent was awfully English but felt that they could have at least appreciated the effort she was making.

Despite the difficulties of her latest visit she enjoyed these trips to the city. She had never ventured anywhere else although had toyed with the idea of revisiting Moscow. She had only been there once and that was on the first of her trips to Russia. Intimidated by the vast metropolis she had never dared making the trip again. Living with Russian families was an adventure that could not be undertaken in a large city where everything was far away and unfamiliar. At least St Petersburg looked like a European city that perhaps not similar to London but what she recalled of Paris and what she had seen of Amsterdam in the travel programs on television that she always watched. The language was different but that was the case even if you crossed the channel.

Joan was defensive in expounding her unhappiness. She loved going home but not until she was ready. She had to prepare herself for the trip back. The one month that she had spent in St Petersburg may not have been ideal but she had visited the Hermitage, been to St Isaacs, visited the Versailles of the north and tried the Russian culinary delights of Borsch, cured meats and cheeses. All these with guides she had hired by the day at a cost of what one private Russian lesson in London would cost. It was like having nephews and nieces all over again, young, grateful for presents and eager to please.

Joan was going home. The flat would be as she had left it. She would go shopping to buy her tins of food. She would watch television and read the paper and wait for someone to call.

*   *   *

Lonely World

It was a hard thing to do. Leave him, I mean. After all I had spent nine years with him and he had become some-one I had relied on to always be there. I had a fear that my world would end and it did. The pain has not really gone but lives just under the surface. I know that is true because I still have moments when I almost lose control. In the middle of the night I reach out for him and wake up with a start on finding he is not there. It is strange because that didn't happen when he would go off on a business trip, sometimes for days on end. I blame myself of course but it hurts that I know I am right to do so. There was obviously something missing and that is why it ended. It is not easy to live with knowing that especially when I had no idea that it was about to happen. I know 'chat shows' often broach the subject with 'show business seriousness' and it is almost a cliché to say that the stu-pid woman should have seen it coming. I don't agree with them.

I once watched a reality show which had private detec-tives capturing the infidelity on video film. I remember no-ticing one of them smiling when talking about the 'poor husband' going to pieces on being presented with the evi-dence. I asked Simon whether he noticed it too but he was reading the paper. He always scowled at my stupidity at watching such programs. He was clever and I always felt that he reminded me I was not with that scowl of his.

It started in the spring, the year before last. His com-pany had just opened a new office in Manchester and he had been given responsibility for ensuring that it had a successful start. The trip was a long trip to begin with. I did offer to join him but he said that he would be all right. It was only three weeks and he would try and make it in between. Manchester is not far from London really and I was surprised when he said that he wouldn't be able to come down for a weekend in the middle of the trip. He rang me nearly every day. I know it started then because he told me. It was my fault.

I suppose not having children might have brought it along. It wasn't that I didn't want children. I did. Simon thought we would have plenty of time and after a row or two I stopped raising the subject.

I haven't stopped crying really. The tears fall, sometimes unexpectedly, but I suspect that I will end up crying as I tell you my story. I am not sure why you would want to hear it. People are getting divorced all the time and so I do not think that there is anything new I have to say.

It was only last month when I found out the truth. Looking back there had been a lot of evidence that something was wrong and something may be going on but I had convinced myself that it was just my imagination. The clearest evidence was last Christmas. I was surprised when he told me that he had to drive up to Manchester on Boxing Day. I couldn't understand why. After all everything closed down for Christmas. He said that there was a problem with the accounting and he had to get everything ready for the auditors. It was unpleasant but plausible. He said it would be a good chance for me to spend some time with my sister. He knew we didn't get on but Christmas was a 'season of goodwill to all men' and anyway it would be a nice thing to do.

I asked him why anyone would be at work but then I never understood his work and he reminded me.

I rang him at work the next day and the receptionist said that there was no one around.

He rang later that day to say that he missed me. He said that the receptionist was a relief receptionist and wouldn't have known he was in. It was a few days later that I remembered that he said everyone had to register at reception. He said he didn't and got angry. We had a row. I asked him point blank whether he was lying to me and he swore that he was not. He accused me of suspecting him of having an affair. I asked him whether he was and he denied it. That night we made love and I felt something different. Each time he said I was beautiful in my heart I heard him saying it to someone else.

He brought a photograph home with him of that Boxing Day dinner. It looked like a party. They all seemed to be enjoying themselves. I was hurt. I wanted to be at that party. I didn't go to my sisters after all. I stayed at home and watched television waiting for him to telephone. I joked about the girl he was standing next to. I said that she was standing a bit too close for my liking. We laughed it off, then.

It wasn't until the spring that I knew something was different. He started picking fights with me. I didn't know what I was doing wrong. I thought he was under pressure at work and I needed to make allowances for him. It wasn't easy. He stopped ringing me as often as he had. We didn't make love as often as we did before and when we did it was predictable. I didn't really enjoy it anymore. I suppose there was something that just didn't feel right. I asked him whether it was all right for him and he said it was. I let it go thinking that we probably needed a break. He was too busy. The Manchester project as it had now become known at home had blown up and he was working at weekends as well. Apparently, the auditors had detected a large number of weaknesses in the systems that needed to be sorted out before the next year-end.

I found out last month. I rang his office in Manchester and they said that he had not been in. I didn't say anything to him at the time. He then left for Manchester again. I said I would call him and he said not to bother. He would be difficult to reach but I did.

When he got back from Manchester I asked him. It was late and he was tired. I could see that but I had not slept for days. I was exhausted.

'Simon, I know you are having an affair. I need to know the truth! You have got to tell me the truth!'

I don't why he had to tell me.

'Yes. I am sorry.' He said.

I was beside myself. I didn't know what else to do except cry. I kept asking him why. I just wanted him to tell me why? I don't know how that would have made me feel any better. I had this idea that if I knew why then I would make sure that similar circumstances wouldn't arise again. That way he wouldn't have to have an affair again, would he? That was the idea.

He told me he was sorry over and over again. He said he loved me and wanted to be with me and no one else. He said he didn't know why it happened. He promised he had ended it on his last trip. He said that it was all in the past and that we could go back to how things had been.

I was afraid. I needed Simon. I tried to put it out of my mind. We made love after a few days but it was disgusting. I didn't say anything at the time. All I could imagine was how it had been like with the other woman. It was the girl he had stood close to in the photograph. She was younger of course. I thought the sex we had was good. The next day when he got home I started crying. I said that I was going mad. All I kept thinking about was the betrayal. I asked him how he could have said he loved me if he could betray me. He said I was being silly, childish. It was just sex he said but why could he not have had the sex he wanted with me. After all I was his wife and isn't that what wives are there for.

I cried myself to sleep that night. He was annoyed with me.

Two days later I did it again. He got really angry. Started shouting at me. He said that there was nothing that he could do to wind the clock back. What had happened had happened. I was the one who had to deal with it. When I asked him how I could be sure it would not happen again he said he promised. There was nothing more he could do. It was my problem and I had to deal with it.

I did. It was a month ago. I told him that he should come and take his things. I said that I was not able to deal with this. He was good. I told him to come when I was out. He tried to ring me once but I told him I didn't want to talk to him. He is probably with that tart in Manchester. I wish I had her telephone number so that I could ring her and tell her it is not her fault. Tell her that I wish she had thought of how I would feel before she allowed it to happen. I wish I had burnt the 'Boxing Day' photograph.

Friends at work say that the pain will pass with time. I don't think it will. I want it to because at the moment I can't sleep. I have cried myself to sleep every night.

I want him to ring me. I want him to come home and tell me it is all over. I want him to come and tell me that he made a mistake and that he still loves me. I want him back with me although I know that if he did I would start wondering when the next time would happen. How could I ever be sure?

I know that there is nothing new in the emotion. I know the chat show hostess will ignore this one but this is real.

I suppose we will go through a divorce. I don't know what he will do. I hope he will not fight about the house. I will let him have it if he agrees to help me find a little place of my own. I don't want to live here anyway. I hate each room. I want to change everything and have done so several times but somehow it still looks the same.

My sister who is now talking to me said that if I was going to behave the way I am why did I ask him to leave. I wish I hadn't but how would I have been able to live with him. I had never betrayed him. I love him. He always said that he loved me more than I could ever love him and I believed him. Now I know that I love him more than he ever loved me. I wonder whether he ever loved me. I tried to remember yesterday what it had been like at the beginning but the only thing I remember is that he was so tender I thought no one could love me more than Simon did.

I wish I hadn't asked him to leave. I wish he was here with me. I wish he was here to tell me that he would always be with me. I wish he would tell me he loved me and I would believe him. I wish I had the courage to ring him and tell him to come home. I know he would.

*   *   *

My Angels

I

The world is full of people trying to cope with the trials of life. Never quite achieving the release they so desperately need, many resort to the numbness that routine has to offer. That is how they pass through the precious years without having to acknowledge the failure that is as much an incumbent of life as is the momentary deceit of success. More real than the futility of achievement in their humdrum existence is the exaggeration that they use to fool themselves into believing that there is something real. It is not the real pain of a life of disability but more the psychological distortion of reality brought about by the illusion of happiness.

I spoke to angels when I was young and they left me when I chose to face the reality of this existence. The pleasure of ignorance bored me and I shunned it despite the warnings that writers before me had stated in the most graphic of detail. I saw the heavens once as clearly as I see day and night. The heavens had no stars, no meteorites, no sun, no moon but a natural beauty that was not born of any physical phenomena. There was nothing artificial about it, no opposites to provide a reference point for our mortal understanding. The angels were not good or bad but simply angels, pure and blissful beings that existed because they were willed to be.

The colours of heaven did not need rainbows to express delight, they rose through the light so bright that I could see nothing but the magic of nothingness. The will to create gave birth to sounds that merged the senses of smell and touch and I drowned in them with a pleasure that continued as an unending crescendo that peaks and is held there moving in motionless ecstasy.

I gave all that up because I chose something different. Perhaps I was not able to contain the excitement of being at one with the angels. Whatever the reason I chose and fell to earth.

Wandering through the quagmire of life, of relationships, of physical disabilities and psychological inadequacies I found my being empty and alone. I tired of the sensations that communication brought me because I found they brought me nothing more than a temporary blindness and begging for the ever lasting blindness that Oedipus had to shield himself from truth I resorted to choices that gave me pain.

I was thirty years old when I realised that there was not much more I could hope for and the prospect of another forty years of torment filled me with horror.

I saw the indulgence of man with wars and starvation, with games of power, with measures of success and failure all of which led to nothing more than the passage of time. A nose bleed let me dramatise the mucus flowing from my nostrils much to the shock of those around me and I encouraged that reaction with the flow of drugs that caused more admonishment than physical pain.

I laughed at the way society couldn't cope with seeing my self-flagellation and do-gooders trying to redeem me by giving me good drugs instead of bad ones. I was described as one who was prone to suicide which excuse they used to incarcerate me for my own good as if I didn't realise that it was nothing more than giving them an excuse to hide behind those who had the authenticity to collude with impunity. Doctors who had little time and even less desire to ascertain what might be the problem held me down until they could certify me as being unacceptable for social interaction.

It was in the darkness of that solitude they imposed that I saw my angels again, bright in that light which pierced through my skin as the shroud of resurrection. I rejoiced in finding my angels again and sent them to you because you were in pain. I didn't know why. You would not say, but I knew you were in pain so I gave them up to you. They asked why but I did not answer because that would have betrayed my desire for you and I was not prepared to do that.

They asked if I was sure this time and I said that I was. I said that I was on my way home and had no need of them. They asked me once more and I wondered whether maybe this time it would be a mistake but then I heard your voice and I was sure. I told them to go and kiss your eyes and whisper comfort in your ears and hold you with the tenderness that passion has never felt. They are my angels and they cared for me. I missed them desperately but knew that was the right thing to do because you needed them.

You did not trust me. You did not believe me. You thought I may have been lying to you but because I thought you had the greater need I forgave you. I wanted the doubt to be removed but you wouldn't let me. You wouldn't let me share your pain so I gave up the only truth I had for you.

I fell again after that night. I didn't hear them any more. The light disappeared and I was left alone. I knew I could not fight to live or determine death. You thought you were being kind to let me exist and I showed gratitude because you were there in my loneliness.

You left with my angels and didn't call. You said that there were things that you needed to sort out. You said you had a life to live and the pain you felt would help you feel the life that my angels couldn't give you but you wouldn't return them to me.

You left me your voice ringing in my ears that silenced any protest that I may have made and I accepted the good drugs that made those around me feel comfortable in their sadness.

'He was a bright child, intelligent and always interesting. We can't think what went wrong and Doctors try different tests to find the cause.'

No one asked me. If they had I would have answered. I would have told them why I was sad. I would have wept the tears that Lucifer will cry on the day that ends all days. I would have told them that it started the day my angels left me. The first time when I fell to earth and then when I wanted to show you how much I needed you. I would have shared my failure, my loss of innocence which made subsequent falls from grace easier.

II

It was a cold night and I wet myself. The warmth was worth more than the smell could take away so I didn't get up as my Mummy had told me to. I knew she would be annoyed but that would be later so for now it didn't matter. I knew she loved me and therefore her anger would not last forever.

My father hit me but that didn't matter. I was glad because my Mummy wouldn't get annoyed. Instead she would shout at him and I would be saved. He would hit her and that would make me sad but he never looked for excuses. I told my Mummy not to worry because I spoke to angels. She wept with me but I don't think she believed me.

I saw the bruises and felt sad but I did not feel the pain. I tried to feel but in those days, before you came along, I was a child and that was the excuse I used to get through the moments of uncertainty. I used extremes of emotions to hide my fear of betraying what I did not understand. They would remain with me for those formative years, those years when I hid my angels away so no one would see them, and no one did. They were nice angels because they loved me. No one believed me when I told them. At first I was sad but then when I found that it was no use I realised that I could still be happy. It became a game I played. I would tell the truth and no one would believe me and so my secret was safe no matter what I did.

And then, after all those years of waiting, you came along. I thought I would tell you about them but I wasn't sure. You were young then and unsure of what relationships meant. You had played games of love and along the way had forgotten about the dream of forever. I still knew how to dream as I was pure. In my garden my angels lived the carefree life of innocence. I was not sure about you and they warned me. The voices in my head told me to play it safe and I did for a while although each time you came close to me I wanted to let you into my secret world where forever was a reality that none but I knew.

You said that you would never hurt me and yet each night while I waited for you to ring I cried because the pain was unbearable. The voices pounded in my head like a hammer smashing my brain until the memory of why I was waiting vanished. Breathless I would fall onto my bed, my phone in my hand and yet you still played the waiting game. You slept while I waited. You met friends while I waited. You stayed away until I saw you the next day and you smiled as if nothing had happened. I took the drug and forgot what had happened the night before and asked if I could ring you. You said I could and then sent me an SMS saying that you were tired and were going to bed and could I ring tomorrow. I tried to stop waiting but then when I got home it started again. I wanted to ring you but couldn't because you said that you would be sleeping. The next day your smile came in like the tide and, just as I got ready to swim out, it receded.

'We will be friends' you said, 'just friends.'

I didn't want to be friends. I wanted the dream of forever with you. I wanted to share my angels with you and all you could say was 'Let's be friends.' The pounding became unbearable. Each night in the middle of the night, in the middle of an unremembered nightmare I would wake up with blood on my pillow. My brain pissed itself through my nose and I wiped it on my face as if it were the blood of some ritual sacrifice. The taste of that sacrificial blood salted with my tears quenched my thirst and I fell asleep again. On the fifth night of that holy week I let you go. You wanted to be friends with me and so I let you go.

I stared a lot at the television. That is what crazy people do. I saw it in a film once. Everyone believed me. Everyone thought I was watching the shit that entertained all those failures that had given up on the dream. Ha ha! Very funny! Such crap and all they did, those normal people, was to kill the time that stood between them and death. Morons! Each and every one except you, Mum! You were always good to me, always feeling sorry for bringing me into this world. I told you not to worry. I wanted you to know that I forgave you. I told you once but you didn't understand. I forgave you, Mum, but I would never forgive anyone else.

Mum, you cried when they committed me again. I didn't mind. They left me in a padded cell which allowed no noise to escape and I screamed obscenities until I was hoarse. I cried till I could cry no more. They gave me good drugs to calm me down. I slept longer than I was awake and, after I had destroyed time, I prayed.

You always cried when you saw me. The guilt you carried with you must have been enormous. Bigger than the pouch in which you carried my life form for nine solitary months. I wanted to cry when they told me that you had died but couldn't. The loss was greater than any display of emotion could hope to equal. I didn't come to your funeral. They said I was there but I wasn't. I know because I would have known if I had been there. Maybe then I would have cried. They said that I was drugged and that is why I couldn't remember. They always dreamed up explanations to cover up their inadequacies.

I got bored with the padded cell and decided to leave. I stopped being myself. They said that the treatment was working but the truth is that I just got bored. Dad came to get me when I was released. He couldn't feed me so they sent the home help along each day to feed me. I didn't like her so I started feeding myself. The same went for changing my clothes or wiping the shit. I decided to live like Dad wanted me to. I kept asking for you but Dad said that you had gone away. I knew you had died but I wanted to hurt him. I wanted to remind him that he should have died, not you, Mum.

I started working at the supermarket helping those old people who couldn't look after themselves. It was voluntary work which meant that I didn't get paid. Dad and the social worker told me to be grateful that the supermarket had given me a job. It was OK. I pushed trolleys around for people who thought that they had the right to tell me what to do. They said they were doing me a favour but that was not true. I got to know the ones that were nasty and I spat on their groceries when they were not looking. I got to know what they wanted and put shit into their food without getting caught. I hoped they would die and, as they took their last breath, know that it was the fool they pushed around that had willed their death. I made Dad tea and spat in it. He didn't notice but I knew and that was the secret revenge of all those beatings that he gave you, Mum.

I was lying in the road looking at faces around me. Everyone telling everyone else what they should be doing.

'Give him air! Don't move him! I think he is alright! He might have broken his neck! Call an ambulance! Is there a doctor here?'

They wouldn't let me die with all their babbling! The sound of the siren woke me up and they were sitting there beside me. My darling angels! After all this time they finally came back to me and I knew that my life would be good again, like it was when I was little. Like when Mum used to go to work and leave me with my angels and I was happy again. I didn't tell anyone about my angels. It was a secret. I had told Mum but she was dead and so my secret was safe.

You came to see me when you heard about the accident. You kissed me on the forehead and called me sweetheart and I believed you.

You looked liked shit! Like a slut that had long passed her 'sell by date'. You cried when you saw me and it sounded just like Mum. You told me that you missed me and wanted to be my friend again.

I asked you what had happened but you told me that you couldn't tell me because we didn't know each other well enough. You said that you didn't want to hurt me. You lied to me again but I believed you. You whore, you lousy bitch, but still I believed you. My angels sat on the bed and tried to tell me but I didn't want to listen to them.

You had a scar near your ear which was new. You said that things would be different this time and I let you stay. I asked you about the scar and you said it was experience.

You came home with me. I was glad because I didn't know what to do when Dad died. You called the ambulance and pushed my wheelchair at the funeral. You came home with me again and slept with me to comfort me. You were good in bed although you stank! It was free so I didn't care. You said you needed me so I let you stay. It was nice to have someone else having nightmares for a change. You were weak and I felt strong and so I loved you. I sent you my angels and you thanked me for them. I ordered them to kiss your eyes so that you would sleep and they did. My angels looked after you. I missed them but let them stay with you each time you went out.

One day you didn't come back. I thought you had died but you sent me an SMS. You said you wouldn't give me back my angels. You said they were yours. You said that they were payment for all the time you had spent with me. I panicked in disbelief and then remembered. It was OK. I had been there before. I knew that they would come back the way cats and dogs do. They know where home is. You told me that you loved me and missed me and couldn't live without me and I gave you my dream of forever in return. I gave you my angels to look after the dream but you didn't look after them, did you? That is why you cried.

III

Forever is here in the silence of the everlasting light. My angels play with me and Mum is here too. I have forgiven Dad and he is good again as he was when he first met Mum. We all live in the dream of forever, happy, until Lucifer is hanged!

*   *   *

My Hero

'People are falling in love all the time and it makes me wonder what the hell this emotion is that causes so much uncertainty in what is already an uncertain enough life.'

Of course I do not quote Jeremy exactly. He is neither famous enough to be quoted exactly nor clever enough to be plagiarised but I like the sentiment because it is one of those that rings true in the life of a voyeur and confirmed bachelor such as myself.

I see poor souls falling in love all over the place, and then suffering the withdrawal symptoms of falling out of love. Like Jeremy, I feel sorry for them all.

Jeremy was a clever old school friend of mine who always took chances and always seemed to come out on top. He was tall, a little under six feet, blonde with a good head of hair and of an athletic build that one secretly envied. He was of course extremely sought after by the opposite sex which, for all the public denials that women make about not being charmed by good looks, meant that he had choice, the one thing that most of us don't have. I think it was that choice that made him naturally unfaithful and the idea of love was still born in him.

I was a romantic as many of us are at school and even though Jeremy would often tease me about it, I loved being around him. I think it was his confidence that we admired as well as of course stories of his affairs that provided us with the subject matter of sexual fantasy.

We kept in touch through university although we found places at different ends of the country and then by telephone through the early part of our careers. I say we kept in touch but in truth I should admit that it was I that called him more often that he called me.

Unable to form long lasting relationships with girls that had resulted in painful love affairs I had decided that love was something that would find me in time and not the other way around. In the meantime I had determined to live the life of a bachelor, which, for me, was having a circle of friends and ensuring that my social life was as full as I wanted it to be. Holding myself out to be a romantic I developed an interest in music; Wagner, and literature; Proust that together provided me with an introduction to a determined group of people that benefited from the emotional security such myopic interests offer.

Jeremy was not the sort of person who would have fitted in with the group that believed seriousness was a prerequisite of being cultured. His flippant attitude to life was something that my fellow Wagnerians would have found commonplace and although I would have to agree with them for my sense of security and purpose I was still envious of the life that Jeremy talked so much about. If he had agreed to be my friend as I certainly was his I would, I think, have given up Wagner and Proust, but then I would have done so only if I was absolutely sure. Thankfully Jeremy never gave me any indication that such total dedication was required. He always found time to speak to me on the telephone and although his social life did not allow us much opportunity to meet in person, his occasional invitations to dinner parties were accepted as adequate reciprocation of the friendship that I had for him.

His marriage was exactly the sort of marriage I expected him to have, a church wedding in a picturesque Sussex village to a daughter of someone who thought it only proper to pay to have his daughters engagement and marriage advertised with a studio photograph in Country Life.

Susan, his fiancée and then his wife, was an English girl with the good looks that money could buy. I wasn't chosen as best man, for which Jeremy apologised.

I resented the fact that after his marriage I lost contact with him. He stopped returning my calls and I turned more to my own circle of friends to allow our friendship pass into memory. I continued to remain true to my belief that I was the ultimate romantic and therefore barred from ever experiencing true love in this life. I imagined permanent relationships with a number of women but then always found fault with them at an early enough stage to ensure that no relationship developed to the extent that it could cause disappointment to either party.

It was with some surprise that I took Susan's telephone call and accepted an invitation to meet for lunch next time she was in London. We agreed to meet at a restaurant not far from my office. I also, as requested, agreed not to tell Jeremy about the meeting.

Susan was already waiting for me by the time I got to the restaurant. She looked as if she had been waiting for sometime.

'Thank you for agreeing to see me, Alex.'

'Sorry I'm late,' I said for want of something to say even though I was not. I had not met Susan after the wedding and it was only by looking up her photograph in an old Country Life that I was able to remind myself of what she looked like. She had aged in the three years of her marriage.

We ordered from the menu limiting ourselves to a main course. Susan, it was clear, was not interested in eating.

'I called you because I know you and Jeremy are old friends. I wanted to talk to someone who knows Jeremy well and also knows how he would react in certain situations.'

I wanted to say something but understood that Susan wanted to speak, not answer questions.

'You know I met Jeremy at the horse trials at Chester. He is so handsome, isn't he? He came up to me with a glass of champagne. 'I thought you could do with some champagne,' he said ignoring my friends completely. I don't know why I accepted the glass. Maybe it was his confidence. I was a little embarrassed at first but he makes it all so easy. I am sure you know what I mean.'

I knew exactly what she meant. Jeremy had the knack of assuming he had the right to intrude on any conversation and always got away with it.

'You have known him for a long time. Do you think he loves me?'

I was about to give her a stock answer 'Why of course he does! What ever gave you the idea that he doesn't!' and other such exclamations one is brought up with through an education of pulp fiction and Hollywood movies but Susan thankfully continued....

'I don't think he loves me and wanted to ask you, as his friend, do you think I would be betraying him if I left him.'

The silence that followed was one that I wanted her to fill. I thought about my friend, the awkwardness that I had been placed in and wishing that I had never agreed to this meeting. I missed Jeremy and I had thought that this meeting with his wife would be a way of getting him to rekindle the friendship that we had before he got married. I had been troubled by the request that I should not tell Jeremy about our planned meeting but thought Susan wanted to buy Jeremy a surprise gift. In fact, I had been flattered by the fact that she had chosen me. Funny how I had not checked with Susan why she did not want me to tell Jeremy about our proposed meeting.

'Why would you want to leave him?'

Susan let the waiter serve us.

'I don't know,' she said, 'he makes me so angry. He goes off on these long business trips, doesn't telephone for days at a time and explains it all by saying that he was busy with work. Two minutes is all it takes! Just to say hello, how are you, love you. I can't believe that he can be so busy that he can't find the time to ring me every day. Oh God, I know he doesn't love me.'

Susan pulled out a handkerchief to wipe her nose. I felt sorry for her. I knew Jeremy could be insensitive and felt sorry for her. I think I felt sorrier for her because I could understand exactly how she felt. I remember how Jeremy never apologised for not returning my calls and listening to Susan I realised that hurt me too. Struggling to find something to say I thought it best to let Susan say something else. It was a long silence and I felt cruel for letting her suffer.

'I am so lonely. I am even lonelier than I was before I got married.'

'Susan,' I relented, 'you must have a lot of friends. Why don't you enjoy the freedom of meeting with them? You have a job, why don't you enjoy being a career girl? An ordinary marriage doesn't allow those things. You are well off enough to do what you want to, why don't you enjoy it?'

Multiple questions are a sign of nervousness. I was nervous and clearly out of my emotional depth. I did not want to be in the situation I was in but did not know how I could either help or get out of it without embarrassment to us both.

'My friends are all married and busy with husbands and children. Those that are not, are busy with boyfriends or trying out one-night stands in the hope of finding something permanent. Even my divorced friends are young enough to be looking for a replacement. You see it is not that easy?'

I knew it wasn't. That is why I had resorted to the help of Wagner and Proust, two people who had a following that transcended the politics of aimless social interaction.

'Do you think he will think I am betraying him?'

I wasn't sure whether Susan was concerned with what Jeremy would think or whether she was looking for my approval. Either way the question did not make sense and I resorted to the template used in such circumstances.

'Have you found someone else?'

Susan didn't reply immediately. I concluded that she must have. She had betrayed him. I imagined her with her mysterious lover with Jeremy and myself looking on. My hand on Jeremy's shoulder for comfort. I imagined it as a dirty love making with Susan dominating which was something she would never have been able to do with Jeremy. I imagined a tear that became real and fell onto her napkin. I tried to help.

'Look, Susan, if you haven't fallen in love then it is not a betrayal.'

I imagined her seeing Jeremy and pleading with him to forgive her. She had not betrayed Jeremy for love. She wanted to be with Jeremy forever. She had only ever loved Jeremy. If it wasn't love it was not a betrayal.

'How can you tell whether you are in love?'

There are questions that do not deserve an answer yet we spend our lives devising what, in the circumstances, may be plausible answers. Struggling against that inevitability I though of something to say. Nothing seemed right.

Was it when time stands still, when the full moon shines because you are in love and not because of any astronomical explanation, when you have a feeling that you cannot describe, when you feel totally helpless without acknowledgement of that fact, when it is the only word that may hold any currency in that situation, when you need the help of someone to restore the balance that your life once had, when you decide that you cannot do it alone any more, when you are too scared of failure to have another go.

'People only know that they are in love when the loneliness of not believing it is too much to bear.'

A long silence followed. I struggled to find something else to say. I was surprised I had said what I did.

Susan wiped the corner of her mouth with the napkin, folded it neatly and placed it on the table.

'I am sorry Susan, I didn't mean it.'

We did not end the conversation. Susan stared at the untouched plate in front of her for what seemed like an age and then stood up without looking in my direction and left.

I felt awkward for a moment. I wasn't sure whether she had gone to freshen up or left the restaurant. The waiter came over a few minutes later with a message from Susan to say that she was leaving.

It didn't seem the right sort of ending to either lunch or our conversation. I expected some gratitude for meeting for lunch followed by a promise not to mention anything to Jeremy. Perhaps even a clue as to what Susan was going to do next.

I thought about ringing Susan but the risk of Jeremy

being there didn't allow me the opportunity. Not having spoken to Jeremy since his marriage and never having met his wife after their marriage didn't give me an opening to ask to speak to her.

I thought about ringing Jeremy but there again I would have to admit to a secret meeting with his wife and no amount of denial of having an affair with Susan would be sufficient.

I heard about the divorce from a mutual friend. Jeremy had divorced Susan because he was bored. Jeremy had told him he felt sorry for Susan because he thought it would take her a long time to find someone. The divorce settlement was amicable.

Susan found a plain looking replacement that I knew would satisfy Jeremy's vanity. Susan invited me to her wedding. The couple seemed happy and more importantly they both seemed to be desperately in love.

*   *   *

Nine years old

I

I was nine years old when I received news of my brother's disappearance. He had been on military service and had apparently died in an accident. There was no body to be returned because the mine that had blown him up was not kind. My mother's grief started with a scream that became a wale and lasted for forty days. My father was quiet and resigned in his grief almost as if he had expected something like this to happen. Increasingly young men from our village didn't return and death was not always the cause.

I cried too. I sat with my mother and listened to how God had deserted Muslims around the world. The world was at war and although I couldn't understand why television still showed cartoons I began to accept that this was something I needed to grow up to understand. I also didn't understand what God had to do with it or indeed why my brothers' disappearance meant the persecution of Muslims around the world, but all that was a long time ago.

I know now of the persecution in Iraq of civilians, the torture of prisoners in Afghanistan and the jihad that my Muslim brothers and sisters were conducting in the middle east, in Indonesia and of course here in Britain too. The call to arms, to assert our right to believe in whatever we want to believe in and not be persecuted on account of race or religion was the inalienable right to be free. These were not just slogans. The world, if not affected by the carelessness of my father's generation in terms of global warming was made equally worse by their lack of backbone.

My father's only positive contribution was his emigration to Britain three years before the Iraq war and being granted asylum on account of clever documentary evidence and a healthy dose of good amateur acting. The immigration officer apparently didn't stand a chance. After the initial desperate show of gratitude my father and his friends learned to joke about it. We forgot that we had a better life than we had ever had back at home in Basra. My father's view was Britain was part of the problem we faced during the sanction years and therefore anything we could get in return was our right. He talked about going back after the Iraq war but we never did.

I was not the sort of person that would generally be seen to be associated with any form of extremism not only because I was a girl and seventeen, but also because I was the daughter of a spineless immigrant who knew nothing more than maximising the benefits we received from the Government and someone who had forgotten the true life and had taken to drink. My mother tried to object but my father was stronger than her and it wasn't always easy to hide the bruises when she had to go shopping.

We were a group of nine sisters at school and met at lunchtime and after school in the prayer room that the school had agreed to let us have. We all wore the 'hijab' despite objections raised by the school. It was a girl's school so they would have had a point had it not been for the fact that we had a male teacher and fathers came to pick up daughters after school. It was a victory for the cause.

We had agreed to stop listening to music because it was against Islam and the only thing I overlooked was having my brother's photograph in my bedroom. Of course I hid it when my sisters in Islam came to my house and included that as one of my sins that I asked Allah for forgiveness when I prayed.

I dreamed of love as other girls of my age but that was a love of a righteous man who respected my rights as a woman and did not think of his wife as a slave; someone who would not drink and believed that it was wrong to hit a woman.

I was an Iraqi and proud of it. I wasn't a 'bounty bar' immigrant who had no faith and was doomed to go to hell.

Many of the English girls at school called me an extremist although I did not consider myself as one. I didn't believe in killing people so I did not support terrorists who went around killing innocent people just because they were American or English. I dreamed of a world that was holy, where good people lived and prayed. Like my Muslim sisters I dreamed of making a difference in the world, marrying a good man, bring up children who feared Allah and live the life of a good Muslim.

II

I have grown up now and am married with three children. My father arranged my marriage with a good Muslim who also emigrated from Iraq. He works in the Post office and has a beard and wears is trousers above the ankle that make him look like a lot of Muslim men who are not afraid to show their faith. He prays five times a day and loves the children. He has never hit me and does not drink. He is a good man.

We have a council flat that we bought at a discount because of my husband's income. I originally thought I would work and earn enough money so that we could buy a bigger house but my husband said that showed greed and we should be content with what Allah had provided us.

Our children, Ali, Ayub and Aysha all go to school. Aysha is seven years old and wears trousers under her skirt. Although she is a child she wears a hijab because my husband says it is better that she learns to be a good Muslim from an early age. She cries sometimes because the other children at school make fun of her but my husband tells her it is part of her jihad. She has to learn that the path of righteousness is not an easy one.

The boys are strong and don't have a problem at school. My husband calls them the Mujahidin, which means those who fight for righteousness. It scares me because the world around us knows the Mujahidin as terrorists. I try and tell my husband that he should not talk about fighting because I am afraid of the neighbours. I am all alone at home during the day and sometimes the older school boys and young men in our block of flats shout and scream which also frightens me. I have to go out to do the shopping. My husband uses the car to go to work. He doesn't like me driving. He says that Muslim women should stay at home. I don't mind.

III

Forty days ago was the Thursday that Ali didn't come home from school. He was sometimes late but that day he was later than usual. I always told him that the two brothers should come home together but he didn't always listen. Ayub said that he waited at the gates but got bored so came home.

They found him in a ditch they said. I was only allowed to see his face. His head was covered so I did not see the wound that had caused him to die. I cried. Aysha cried too. My husband was angry but the police said that they could not find out who did it. I heard his body was bruised too. Many people came to mourn with us. I have sat for forty days and cried each time someone came to tell me how sad it is that a little boy should die. They tell me he has gone to heaven. I can only pray that he has.

I don't understand how anything like this can happen. Sometimes I think that we are wrong to wear different clothes in this country but why should clothes make a difference? I ask Allah to give him a place in heaven. I watch television and see clever people talk about fighting for freedom or others about the war on terror and how people must die to save the rest of us from the tyranny of terror. My husband talks about freedom too but I am scared. I don't want freedom. I don't want to make a difference anymore.

Aysha was nine years old when Ali died. I wonder whether she keeps a photograph of her brother.

*   *   *

Piglet

It is true, she actually looked liked a pig the very first time I saw her. Little squinting eyes set in a podgy face and a smile that caused facial distortions that I am sure helped her grunt. That is not to say that she was not beautiful. I know you must think I am mad describing her as beautiful after starting with the statement that she looked like a pig but she did. That is why everyone called her 'Piglet'. She became beautiful when she started going out with me and I punched a good few who made fun of her then. I know I was a bully at school but then why wouldn't I be if I could get away with it.

I didn't like her much at first but after we had been going out for a while I noticed her eyes, grey and blue offset with the dark blackness of the cornea. I had forgotten about Saturday night and didn't have much time to organise a date. It wasn't much fun going to a night club to 'pull' when everyone else was going with their girlfriends so when I saw her at the shopping centre I told her that she was going to go out with me that evening. I wasn't surprised that she said yes as there were not a lot of kids at school who could get away with saying no to me. I knew she would be free because we all had agreed at school that no one would want to go out with her. She said she had a nice time and my friends, after the initial guffawing, thought it was nice of me to take her out. It was an act of christian charity from an atheist. It added to the good humour that the alcohol overlooked.

I wasn't sure what she expected me to do with her afterwards but I was too drunk to be interested and took her home.

After that first date I let her hang around with me and my friends. I taught her how to smoke and get drunk. I was a good influence and I think I made the last year of school fun for her.

I didn't see her for a while after I left school and was

surprised when we ended up in what was called a College of Further Education. There wasn't a lot that one could do with three GCSE's and I decided to learn something. I was going out with Debbie, a firmly built girl who had a sense of fun that encouraged me exactly as my adolescence wanted to be encouraged.

Piglet didn't like me being with Debbie and I remember the fun we had when the two girls fought it out over me. I wasn't there but it was still great hearing about it. Piglet didn't do very well, after all Debbie was at least six inches taller and a good few pounds heavier. Piglet was a mess with two black eyes, a scratch on her cheek and bruises that couldn't be shown to anyone. Debbie was proud of having given Piglet a thrashing and became my sworn enemy when I dumped her for Piglet.

Piglet and I were together for three years. I think if it had been longer we would have moved in together. I didn't understand at first how she could dump me. She had told me that she didn't want to speak to me anymore and didn't want me to come round either so I didn't. After all I had my reputation and it was easy to find someone to replace Piglet. I told my friends that I had given her as much charity as anyone could expect and they all agreed with me. It was about time that I found someone who was worth having rather than go around with someone who would have remained a virgin even if she had lived in a brothel. No one knew that she had dumped me and they will never find out either.

The last time we went out together she was quieter than usual. I thought it must be the time of the month. It didn't matter because we went out in a group and her sulking was easy to ignore. I wanted to ask her what was up but knew that girls have only two answers to questions like that; 'Nothing' or they make something up. I got over Piglet quite easily.

On the way to her house we dropped in at my place for a quick one. Piglet didn't mind and it was over before I had really got started. The beer didn't help. As always, at moments like that, I felt sick. After all it is not much fun on your own and quite honestly you might as well be. She didn't say much. I noticed that she didn't even kiss me back but that never bothered me when I needed it.

I took her home and as I was about to leave, she spoke. I knew I should have taken her home earlier as soon as she opened that mouth of hers.

'You don't really love me do you, Alex?'

She knew I hated her using that word. I always associated the use of the word 'love' with 'girly' films that you tolerated when there was a promise of dessert. I didn't like Piglet using that word and had told her early on in our relationship. Don't get me wrong, I understand that is what girls need and I don't mind it from others but not Piglet.

'Why don't you shut up, Piglet? I know you are having a bad day but that doesn't mean that I need to as well!'

Perhaps that was a little insensitive but it didn't feel like it at the time. Piglet just turned around and went in doors. I was annoyed. After all it wasn't my fault that she was having a bad day. I wondered whether she was crying.

I didn't ring her for the rest of the week but was surprised that she didn't ring me. Friday evening I gave her a call. Her mum said that she wasn't in but didn't say where she had gone. I left a message but didn't wait for her to call. I am sure that she must have called but you can't tell on my telephone. I went out to the pub where my mates were and we had a laugh. They asked me where Piglet was and I made some macho remark about needing a break. Tracy asked me whether she was the break that I had in mind and we went back to her place. She was a lot more fun, had her own place and I knew she had fancied me for a long time. We met again on Saturday night and this time I stayed over at her place.

It wasn't until Sunday night that I called Piglet up again. Her mum said that she was asleep and that she wouldn't wake her. She was a right cow, her mum.

I didn't sleep very well that night and if Tracy had not been on night shift I would have telephoned her. I felt something was wrong but couldn't guess what it could be. I was worried the second time when I couldn't get Piglet at work.

I know it sounds crazy but I actually took time off to try and meet the bitch at work. I went to reception and sent her a message that I was waiting for her. I waited a bloody hour for her. She finally turned up.

'Hi, Piglet, are you OK?'

'Hi Alex.'

That was all. We met as if we were strangers.

We left the building and walked through the park to the tube station. Piglet was quiet. Now that I remember it was the first time that I had ever felt uncomfortable about being with Piglet. I was unsure of myself. Piglet seemed to be in control and I waited for her to say something. It wasn't that I didn't have anything to say. I wanted to ask her why she hadn't telephoned me, why she wasn't at home when I called, where she had been, and suddenly I stopped thinking about it when I wanted to ask her who she had been with.

She suddenly changed direction and walked over to a bench and sat down. I followed and quietly sat down beside her.

'Alex, there is something I have to tell you.'

My mind raced through all the possibilities, skipping over the one that was the most obvious.

'I've been seeing John.'

He was the son-of-bitch that had got to Piglet before me. I remember my surprise at finding out that Piglet was not a virgin and she had mentioned that John had got there before me.

I wanted to say something but didn't know what to say. I wanted to punch her in the face and then fuck her there and then in the park in front of everyone for the slut she was but my thoughts were caught in a net. I remember thinking that I knew what fish felt like. I got up feeling like a complete fool at not being able to say anything. A few parting words would have been sufficient. I wanted to swear at her, something, anything would have been better than nothing! I opened my mouth only to gulp the musty autumn air still staring at her, turned away from her and walked off.

I waited to hear her call out to me and listened hard. I am sure she must have and I just didn't hear it. I waited for her to ring me every day for the next few weeks. I made up for it getting drunk with the lads and having fun with Tracy. Piglet never called. She was a strange one. You can never figure them out.

*   *   *

Shoes

I

She had always had a shoe fetish. It was almost the first thing that Paul had noticed. Not something that he would have noticed himself but something that Jane had made very obvious to him at their very first meeting. The rain had not helped despite the careful choice of restaurant and the nightclub that had been chosen to impress. Jane had spent the whole evening worrying about her shoes and blaming the weather forecast for their consistent unreliability. They were Italian suede slip-ons that were made for the rich that could afford rain damage and not for the likes of Jane who came from a working class family that had always spent wisely.

Jane had always hated the hand-me-down system adopted by her family. She had resented the patronising attitude of her elder sisters from the start. Jane was bright and even though she treated her studies with the same contempt shown by her sisters she still managed to do reasonably well. Even though she had left school as soon as she could she managed to get a job in the design department of a provincial fashion house. Her first pay packet was spent on a pair of shoes without leaving the five pounds a week that she had promised her mother for house-keeping to match the contributions made by her less fortunate sisters.

Jane's move to a London minor fashion house was the liberation that she needed. Starting off in a flat share she quickly moved into a small one bedroom flat of her own justifying the sacrifice of the reduced disposable income that she would have by not having to find new excuses to avoid sharing her clothes and what was even worse, her shoes.

Jane was attractive and Paul's male instinct had blinded him to her eccentricities. Never having had a sister Paul believed Jane's behaviour to be normal for girls. The fact that his previous girlfriends had a collection of shoes larger than he thought was necessary reinforced his view. Even though he had to admit there were moments when he thought she was being a little obsessive he always found excuses for her. After all he had not had someone to share a life with before and the occasional discomfort was he believed to be the price he should pay for the privilege.

It was shortly after their marriage and their pooling of financial resources that brought him to the realisation that some sort of household management was going to be necessary. Jane was accommodating when it came to such discussions, agreeing to Paul's general guidelines on the importance of saving for a larger house, a new car and holidays that they would spend together. Paul was the sort who was passionate about general plans but short on implementation and Jane's readiness to agree to the general plan for saving was enough to give him the satisfaction that he was making progress.

There was no talk of children after the first row of their marriage. Jane, at twenty-four, believed there would be enough time to think about that and the fact that Paul had just turned thirty didn't seem to be a problem either. Paul thought it best not to press the issue for the time being.

As the relationship grew between them Paul found himself short on expected savings. Money was something that Jane managed badly and the only solution that Paul found was to take over the household budget. A personal allowance was made for Jane which she agreed to keep to and Paul again persuaded himself that a satisfactory solution had been found. Paul was earning a lot more than Jane and the budget agreed with Paul left her no worse off than she had been before their marriage with the additional benefit of not having to worry about the running expenses of the house, car and holidays.

The negotiated peace lasted a few weeks. There were gentle hints at lack of satisfaction with her lot that Paul ignored. She had seen two pairs of shoes that she desperately needed, a desperation supported with childlike arguments that didn't permit adult reasoning.

'I just need them, don't you see? I haven't got shoes like those.'

Counting out the shoes that Jane had didn't help. She just went into a sulk that lasted for two days, emphasised by her sleeping in the lounge. Paul, feeling guilty about the discomfort that he was putting Jane through and if truth be told the absence of the physical comfort of sleeping together, not to mention the occasional sexual encounter that Jane allowed him, all helped persuade him to relent. An afternoon of seeing the girlish joy that Jane exuded shopping for shoes, which Paul bought, left him with an emptiness which no amount of energetic expression of love on Jane's part could fill.

As the months passed by, Paul resigned himself to accepting Jane's fetish for shoes. He accepted the compensation of household peace and the sex that Jane offered in return as the only way things could resolve themselves. The swings of mood as he struggled to make ends meet were what he persuaded himself marriage was all about.

II

It was two years later that the next crisis in their marriage came. Jane had been out at a hen party for one of her friends. Jane knew she had promised not to stay out too long. Paul had worked as late as he could and finally decided to give up the pretence of work and go home. He popped into a bar for a quick drink to kill time and got home just past eleven. The television numbed him as he waited for Jane to call to come and pick her up. The second vodka had the desired effect of sending him to sleep. It was with a stiff neck that he awoke staring at a blank screen. He was still drowsy when he looked at his watch. After a moment or two of focusing on the time and then making sure he had read the time correctly he got up with a start. It was five-thirty in the morning.

His first reaction was that of anger at Jane having allowed him to lie there on the sofa and not even bothering to switch off the television. It wasn't generally like Jane to do that but he had confirmed to himself that Jane was occasionally insensitive. He walked around the flat looking for Jane and after the few seconds that it took he realised that she had not come home. He was annoyed, then worried, then helpless and then imagined her state when she would eventually get home. He thought about ringing the police but the embarrassment of explaining that his wife had gone to a hen party and had not returned was too much. He resolved to sit and wait.

Jane got home shortly after six. Although it was not a long wait Paul's anxiety made it feel a lot longer.

'Do you know what time it is?'

Jane ignored his question. She went to the bathroom and locked the door leaving Paul impotent. He decided to wait for her in the bedroom listening for any sounds that would tell him what she was doing. He heard the toilet being flushed and then the shower. Paul waited fuelling his increasing impatience by feeling sorry for himself at his inability to make an impact in the situation.

He heard the bathroom door open and Jane walk into the lounge. He waited a few minutes to hear what she might be doing. After a silence that he could not decipher he got up to check. Jane had made a bed on the couch.

'What's the matter?' he asked.

Jane said nothing. He repeated the question. Again, silence.

'For God's sake Jane, don't shut me out. What have I done wrong this time?'

'Go away Paul, I just don't want to talk now.'

Paul stomped out of the room not knowing what else to do. He tossed and turned himself to sleep. Jane was still asleep when Paul woke up the next morning. He cooked a breakfast of scrambled eggs and toast and then went in to Jane to tell her breakfast was ready.

Jane got up without saying a word. Breakfast was eaten

in silence. The fear of a weekend of matrimonial tension prevented Paul from aggravating the situation. Jane left the kitchen table to have a shower leaving Paul to wash the dirty dishes which he washed. Not knowing what to do Paul decided to wash the car. Nothing passed between them for the rest of the weekend. Paul still looking for an explanation of the exceptionally late night left any discussion until Jane was ready to talk to him about it. Her timing came as a surprise.

A month of underlying tension passed before she was ready.

'Paul, I have something to tell you. I slept with someone. It was only the once and I am sorry'

Paul looked at her in disbelief. He wanted to say something but couldn't decide what to say first.

'I wanted to tell you because I don't want to live a lie. I love you very much and want you to forgive me. I realise I made a mistake and it will never happen again.'

In the end Paul gave up trying to be original in his reaction and played the part of a cuckolded husband, which, unfortunately, was not notable, neither its preparation nor its execution.

III

Paul did not leave Jane as one might have expected of stereotypes in such situations. He cried to show he was hurt, sulked, picked at his food, didn't sleep, moped at work and accepted with exaggerated reluctance the equally exaggerated show of repentance that Jane now showed him. The tables were turned for a while. Paul was, for a change, in a position of strength, which he secretly enjoyed. No reasons for the betrayal were offered probably because in reality there were none to offer.

The relationship was difficult for a while. Protestations of love were more frequent on both sides and time passed more generously than it had previously. There were moments when something would remind him of what had happened but Jane didn't leave him with much time on his own depriving him of the chance to wallow in the self-pity that often left him distraught. As time passed things became better and there was the thought that perhaps they could put the whole episode in the past but then life does not easily give up such an opportunity to remind us of the inherent weaknesses of relationships.

It was a shopping trip that reminded Paul of the betrayal. Jane had seen some shoes that she wanted and had persuaded Paul to join her on the trip to buy them. Although Jane's collection of shoes had by now become too large for her to remember all the shoes she had, as soon as she showed them to Paul he recognised them.

'Darling, you have a pair in exactly the same style as those, don't you?'

'Yes, I had some but they were ruined so I threw them out.'

A hundred pound pair of shoes seemed too expensive to Paul to have been ruined beyond repair so Paul persisted.

'Darling, why couldn't you have got them repaired?'

'Look, Paul, I told you they were ruined. Do you have to spoil it for me? Why can't you just be happy I found something that I really want?'

Paul didn't ask any more questions. It was only late that night that he remembered when she had last worn those shoes. The love making that had gone before had worn out Jane into a blissful state that she was grateful for.

'Paul, I love you so much.'

'Really darling?'

'Paul, what can I do to make you believe me?'

It took a few seconds silence for Paul to reply.

'You could throw away those shoes that you bought today.'

'Why would I want to do that?'

'Because you love me.'

Jane cuddled up to Paul and kissed him.

'You are silly......... I love you Paul.'

'Me too.'

*   *   *

Solomon

The screaming didn't stop, it only changed pitch! Desperation has a way of making itself heard through a number of subtle inclinations in the voice. The screaming tears at the muscles in the brain with the lack of squeamishness felt by those early surrealist film directors. I must explain.

I have been working at this hospital for the mentally ill, insane if you like, well nothing more than 'nutters' really for over two years now. Solomon was admitted about a year ago and I have had to deal with his shit ever since. It's a job like any other. As the saying goes 'someone's got to do it!' It pays the bills of the little flat in Balham that I rent and I save money on fares because I can walk to work. It takes forty minutes but saves me money. It's a shitty flat. The rent is too high and Balham is not what it used to be.

I used to work at the Bedford Arms. I would tell you where it is because it's a really good pub and still busy after the no-smoking laws but then I suppose you are probably a million miles from Balham and even if you were here you wouldn't go there. I worked in bars for about five years until I just got fed up with the shitty pay and shitty hours and decided to get a normal job. The only one I could get with my two GCSEs was in a hospital which was still more money and easier hours even though there was shift work. The clientele is pretty much the same if you count people who have had one too many to drink.

Solomon was admitted screaming obscenities at everyone. The idiots hadn't sedated him enough before they brought him over and although we managed to overpower him it wasn't pleasant being spat at, kicked and punched. That was before I knew that it was alright to return a punch or two provided you don't get seen and the bruise is where the patients could have inflicted it on themselves. I was given Solomon to look after. In a cell on his own.

He was a strange nut! He either sat on the bed in silence staring beyond everything that was in front him or start screaming; no words, just sounds. In fact the last time I heard him say anything rude was when he first came to stay.

I am not important enough to understand the medical condition he was meant to be suffering from but that doesn't really bother me as I am sure you don't care either. I do know that when he was admitted he was forty-five years old, an alcoholic, never taken drugs, divorced and had only one visitor; a woman claiming to be his wife. One of the nurses told me. He had some family but they never came. They never do. I understand that because people have their own lives to live.

His wife always came alone. I say that because if they were divorced I would have expected her to come with at least another man. He was always especially sedated when she came because we were really scared he might do something although he never did. I always wanted to know whether it was the drugs or whether he wouldn't have done anything without the drugs either. Don't worry, I never found out and although I was dying to know I would never take the chance to lie about giving him the drugs. She talked to him incessantly, nothing about anything really. She came once a month. She wasn't that talkative at first but that always happens; visitors need to get used to the idea that there is someone listening or find that they have to fill the silences patients provide.

Mrs Redman always cried after those visits.

I suppose I was closer to Solomon because he was one of my first patients and although I always wanted to get him back for at least some of the bruises he gave me I did like him. I mean, I wish he didn't scream because when he did, he really didn't sound normal and, to be absolutely honest, it used to really piss me off! Apart from that he is OK, normal really, as normal as you or me.

I couldn't understand why he had been locked up for so long. His wife, I called her Sheba, was a good looking woman, probably around forty. I never found out exactly. She was the nice type. Not stunning but someone you could live with. I liked her. If I was married to her I am sure as hell that I would not have ended up in the nut-house.

From the way she dressed it was clear that they had seen good times and, while he had given up on getting through life the best way he could, she had kept going. Why she hadn't left him I don't know and what surprised me the first time I saw it was that she cried. When I saw her cry like that I felt like going in to Solomon and beating the shit out of him. I didn't though because, well, we don't really do that sort of thing. I mean if your husband, or rather ex goes potty why would you feel sorry for him? She didn't look like the one that left him. I don't know why I thought that but it seemed obvious. Why she had to cry though irritated the hell out of me.

I enjoyed my work. I liked the hospital. It was clean and had the smell of disinfected cleanliness that is disgusting but only until you get used to it. Solomon liked it too. I remember talking to him on the occasions when he couldn't feed himself. He used to spit out what I fed him but I sorted him out. I got a pin and poked him with it each time he spat something out. It was like the experiment with the dog, Pavlov or something. Each time he would make a face I would show him the pin underneath the collar of my white coat. It was clever don't you think? I mean it hurt but didn't leave a mark. The doctors heard that I had managed to control him and the bastards gave me more of him to look after. That's life isn't it? I mean the only reward you get for doing a good job is being shat on even more.

I liked talking to him when he was being fed. I told him what a selfish bastard he was, how ungrateful he was compared to all those starving children in those African countries. He didn't say much, just grunted like the pig he was. I tried to rile him once by asking whether he was really that stupid, didn't he care that his wife might be banging someone else for all the four weeks in between visits? There wasn't much of a reaction. I think maybe he realised that he was the one that was responsible and therefore had no right to complain.

My work did depress me sometimes. I mean seeing all those able people who were selfish, full of their own shit without a care about the world or the millions that were being spent looking after them. Money that could be spent looking after the old folk or saving those battered children from accidental parents or paying underpaid nurses or hospital staff, especially those that had to put up with the sort of shit I did. I mean, we cleaned them, fed them, took their shit and the only retaliation was a pin, and if I had got caught I would have been sacked! That is the injustice of it, don't you think?.

Solomon had enjoyed being housed, fed and clothed for a year without doing a days work and there was me, walking to work to save on fares, living in a damp, rat infested bedsit owned by a money grabbing landlord who didn't care and charged the earth. I told the landlord about the rats and his advice was to buy a rat trap! When I complained about the damp he said that if I complained so much I could leave. Yeah, I would if I could find somewhere cheaper. I barely managed to make ends meet.

I once thought how easy it all was. All you have to do is act like a nut for a while and someone is bound to section you. Doctors would develop theories that were crap and only served the purpose of giving them a job for life while they controlled their patients with drugs that anyone could prescribe. I mean, think about it, if you gave the patients the choice of being shot or being sane you couldn't lose. Those patients that were obviously nutters would choose death and those that were not would quickly recover and go on to live a normal life, find some damp vermin infested flat and a job that no-one else would do, marry, and have some snotty children that would replace them in years to come. The doctors would be out of a job, they could sell the land that the hospital was on to some property developer who could make millions building a home for the homeless. It all makes sense. I mean it's like basic economics isn't it!

God! How I hated the bedsit! I remember when I got that Aussie girl, Jo, interested. I told the cow that we should have gone to her place but no! She insisted on coming back to my place and then wanted gold bloody bath taps! I mean she was too pissed to have noticed anyway. I should have thrown her out instead of letting her stay the night.

'You didn't complain about it last night!'

She called it a pig sty. She had no right. It's my place. I'm allowed to call it anything that I want but she isn't. I didn't see her for about a month after that. I suppose I shouldn't have told her that slag's had no right to complain. I thought it was funny at the time. You should have seen her face. She smashed a few glasses and plates and left. It didn't matter, they were from a boot sale anyway, ten pence each. I got some more the next weekend. I didn't like clearing up the mess but that was alright. It was like being at work. I tidied up before she came over the next time even though she was even more plastered than the first time and I haven't been rude to her anymore. She's OK now, moved in two weeks ago.

I tried to find out about Solomon but the files are confidential. I went into the doctors' room once when I was on the evening shift. Doctors in nut houses have it easy. They don't have to do shifts, not like in normal hospitals.

That Dr Patel is a nutter too. In fact if he wasn't wearing a white coat I swear he could easily have been mistaken for a patient. He's about fifty with an accent that belongs in a curry place. He never combs his hair. I bet he hasn't washed his hair in months! He smells of curry too, eye brows that have grown in all directions, and hair coming out of his nose and ears. He's careless too. He is not allowed to leave files in huge piles on his desk but he does. Someone could report him but he doesn't bother anyone enough to make them do that, he just leers at the nurses, the dirty old bastard. I didn't understand a lot of what was in his files but that was not only because of what was written, you know doctors and their handwriting, you can't read a thing! I think they practice that handwriting because they are shit scared of getting caught for prescribing all the wrong drugs. I mean, it can't be humanly possible to know the names of all those drugs, let alone remember what those drugs do. I once thought it might be fun to give the wrong pill or not give one at all to see whether it made any difference. Don't worry, I didn't! It was just a thought. I mean you understand what I mean, right!

Looking through the file that I saw didn't help me much. Even what was readable was written in shorthand scribbles. I gave up on that way of finding out. I mean I liked Solomon. He was a selfish bastard but that was OK. I have met a few sane ones that are worse. I mean, I told you about my landlord!

What I found out about Solomon was from his wife. I saw her crying one day in the corridor after a visit. She was waiting for a cab. Her car was being serviced.

'Are you alright, Mrs Redman? I'm Wayne. I look after your husband.'

She dried her eyes with one of those tissues that are sold in small packets. You know the ones that cost as much as a big box but fit into a handbag. They are probably scented too. I saw Jo with one once.

'I'm alright. Thank you.'

That was the opener. I told you she was the talkative type.

She lived on her own, they didn't have any children and she was a teacher. Although she said that were not divorced I think she may have been lying. She could only come once a month because she lived a long way away. She didn't say where. I think she was lying. She didn't have the heart to say that there was not much point. She told me that Solomon didn't like children, which was why they didn't have any. He had lost his job in a bank after working there for twenty-two years. His problems had begun after sitting at home for about six months. He had started drinking and wouldn't stop. He started getting violent, breaking things and then hitting her. She had tried make-up but they noticed at the school. She told them that she fell but someone from the school rang the police and he was taken in and sectioned. He blamed her for it but it wasn't her that got him sectioned. I think she was lying.

You know what the best bit about it was? She blamed herself. The bastard screws up his life and hers and she blames herself. Some women really deserve what they get. I can tell you if she were my type I would have been in there no problem. I mean, you can't go wrong with that sort, can you?

I remember talking to Jo about it. Jo said that Solomon was a typical man. I called her a cow for saying so but you know she was right. Well, not all men but there are definitely a lot of the 'Solomon' types.

Mrs Redman said that if she had accepted his drinking maybe all this wouldn't have happened. I told her that from what I knew people don't get sectioned for being alcoholics. It's got to be something else. I told her not to worry and that everything would be alright.

The screaming didn't stop. One day it did change pitch. It was her screaming when the bastard died. He haemorrhaged. Apparently things like that happen too.

*   *   *

That Certain Age

Ralph was reaching that stage in his life when every-thing seemed to have almost passed him by. He was aware of what he was doing thinking like that especially as he had already some months earlier confided that feeling to a friend who, with the reassured confidence of someone who had been through it, had pronounced it to be an ill-ness of men of Ralph's age. This time it was not funny. Ralph had, when younger, turned into a witty remark both senile dementia and mid-life crisis and now that he had been diagnosed as having one of them with the other soon to follow it was no longer funny.

His wife, that tower of strength in more recent years, had been there to console him with desire particularly when after an evening spent having a drink with friends and flirting with waitresses less than half his age ended with the lonely trek home in brooding disappointment. Despite no reciprocal satisfaction his wife still enjoyed mothering him as he lay there spent, wondering what it might have been like had he been with the waitress. Judy, oblivious of the workings of her husbands' dying mind enjoyed the momentary happiness as she filed away the inadequate performance for use at a later date.

Ralph started exploring his biological disintegration with some urgency. After all he was still young. The fifty two years that he had clocked up had sneaked up on him and although his body had suffered the growing pains of decrepitude his mind still burned with the desire to do things, to see things and above all continued to harbour the feeling that death was something that came to other people and he had a long time to wait before he would have to start thinking about it. He was however getting a little anxious, mostly because of people around him. His friends were growing old. They no longer wanted to do things any more and any thought of playing the truant in the school of life met with a "Come on Ralph, act your age!"

He wanted to buy himself a present for all those years of hard work, providing for his family and looking after all those that depended on him with a resigned acceptance of duty. This was the thought he had shared with Joe, his friend of fifteen years or so, when instead of discussing the proverbial Porsche Joe had come out with the diagnosis. He had been startled by it to begin with but then, when calmed into analysis by Joe's concerned seriousness, he found himself looking for a way out rather than admitting to the disease that had developed unnoticed and now signalled the end.

Judy was a lot more supportive. She encouraged him to think of what he would like as a reward and went through the toys that she had heard others desire. A sports car, a barge, a holiday with his friends to some distant country in pursuit of a sporting event or something that appeared to indulge his selfish desire to waste part of what they had spent a lifetime saving. All these indulgences Judy noted excluded her and the children which although a little hurtful if she thought about it was acceptable as something that her mother had put up with which the justification of the creation of the wealth as in the main being his and not hers ended any thoughts of disloyalty on his part.

Ralph was pleased at the approach Judy took. He didn't have to support that desire which, like others of his gender, he believed to be an inalienable right of men to indulge themselves. The question that was more important was how was he going to spoil himself?

He had always had a passion for cars but then as he embraced marriage and then family life he had found his desire to enjoy the 'vroom' of driving fast first handicapped by financial constraints and then later by the responsibility of the lives of his wife and more importantly his daughter. To buy a Porsche now, while a wish that had lingered from his bachelor days, was no longer something he believed he could get away with. Ever since Joe had come up with the diagnosis he had been mulling over the thought of a Porsche but had come to the conclusion that he didn't really want to join the horde of middle-aged men driving a Porsche at thirty miles an hour out of what had become a malignant fear of speed cameras.

Travelling the world, flying to some exciting city with friends seemed excessive as he could very well do that without leaving home and anyway he wouldn't want to spend that much time away from home. It would be fun for a few days but then having already got into the habit of not doing anything like that it had become unthinkable. In any event he knew that by the third day of getting drunk 'with the boys' he would get home sick and sulk for the rest of the trip. The thought of reducing any trip to last for no more than a long weekend seemed not extravagant enough.

Ralph thought at times that he would go mad. He sat in his office looking at the calendar which that reminded him of a regional office review planned at the end of the month. October was not a pleasant month for trips and this was one that his boss had got out of by efficient planning of a late holiday and the obvious delegation that ensued.

October was an unpleasant month. The loss of summer was still fresh, the fear of winter had already set in and Christmas still too far away to provide any comfort. He sat there debating whether he should take a first class train to Oxford or drive up. It was about a hundred and fifty miles and either way would require being away from home for two nights. The thought of being able to drink on the way up and back might be fun but then the flexibility of driving sounded interesting. He liked driving and a three to four hour drive seemed to him on balance to be the preferable option. He planned on doing it during the week so that the weekends would be free. Free to spend time with the family, his wife and daughter enjoying the pleasures of domesticity.

The weekends would be a standard routine, ever since his daughter had reached the age when communication was a trial of patience for both, her demands of an earlier age when friends intervened at the most inconvenient times; Saturday afternoon, Sunday evening or any other time at the weekend meant the world revolved around her. Anything that remained was time for shopping or household jobs which he was equally never inspired to do. Now that she had finished university and was in a job that encouraged financial arrogance she was someone that he liked being with but which he knew she tolerated because of the inability to provide a home for herself. Another year or two and that would no longer be a problem for her and he dreaded the loss that would entail. He had recently bought her a car and knew that once she realized that she could get away with it she would insist on help with buying a house.

Ralph pondered on what his life had become. He wondered how Judy coped but after finding the question too difficult to answer he would always put it down to a gender issue and move onto some other question of life that was easier to contemplate and at the same time of more interest to him.

Judy at the same time had developed into that maternal figure born of years of training provided by Ralph and their daughter. That maternal figure had helped her put her own ambition aside when Clare was born and then cater for the happiness of her family by creating a domestic environment that provided comfort and security away from the torment of the outside world. A world that she had long ago lost the habit of living in and the fear of the new prevented her having any desire of re-entering. She had a husband she understood and a daughter of which she was proud and had long accepted entering middle age with indifference. Some of her friends had moments when they wished life had turned out differently for them but when she had tried to take part in that fantasy she had difficulty in imagining a life different to the one she had been lucky to have.

Ralph tried to get on with life but the question returned more often and like the pains of childbirth it was clear to him that he would end up screaming in fear of the unknown. He wondered whether everyone really did go through this unpleasantness or whether the intensity of the desperation he would feel from time to time was something reserved especially for him.

Through sharp pains of panic his days passed by. Judy worried about him and gave him the special attention she always gave him when he was ill. She entertained him with cooking that came down through the ages of matrimony, allowed him enthusiastic passes to visit friends without her and reconciled herself to allow him to make love to her whenever he wanted to. The last of these was easy as they were not as frequent or demanding as they used to be which was something that had it not been a relief for her, would have worried her.

Ralph left the house early. He hadn't planned it but not having slept well he decided to get out of bed and go into work. He had planned to leave the office after lunch for the drive to Oxford and therefore the extra time he would have in the office would give him the time he needed to make the day a more relaxed one that it would otherwise have been.

Judy was still asleep and he didn't wake her until he was ready to leave. Clare was up but in her room so he shouted a 'Bye Clare' to which he didn't wait for a reply. He had long learned not to expect a reply. To get over the obvious sense of hurt that he had felt when this particular routine had started he made it easy for himself by leaving the house with the thought that had he waited in the house for a reply one would have been received.

The Saab was new and the thought of a long drive excited him. He enjoyed his Rover and although it was a lot cheaper in terms of the personal contribution he was required to make than having a Saab he had decided to treat himself to the most expensive car in the range available to his grade at work. In any event, as he had unnecessarily explained to Judy, it was for both of them. Judy had however never made it clear to him that she liked been driven to the supermarket in the Saab rather than the Rover. Ralph had overlooked her oversight and accepted the notion that she obviously did. Who wouldn't?

Ralph didn't have lunch in the staff canteen. He wasn't hungry and could always stop on the way if he wanted to have something to eat. He worked through lunch and by 3 pm had left the approach to Southampton behind.

The journey was smooth with not much traffic to contend with. There were advantages leaving on a Tuesday. Monday would have been much worse.

He had decided to stay at a motel just outside the city that he had been advised was convenient for the office. He had been to the office many years ago shortly after starting work and had enjoyed the mileage allowance that the opportunity had given him. The luxury then of staying in a hotel where someone else would pick up the expenses gave the visit an excitement that had long since left him. This time he was on his own and his time would no longer be spent on grinding through the numbers but instead having meetings with the heads of the various departments to obtain information to compile an oversight report. Easy work, this was a routine office review that required no more than attendance and the patience of being bored for two days. It was no wonder that his boss had booked the visit during a planned holiday.

He got to the motel shortly before eight. The journey had taken longer than expected because of the lazy breaks for coffee that Ralph had indulged in on the way. He decided to have a shower and then go down to the restaurant to get something to eat. It was too late to go into town and anyway it wasn't much fun going into town on your own. Remembering that he had not had any lunch had made him hungry.

There was no one in the restaurant. He picked a table not far from a piano that occupied the centre of the restaurant. It was very much a no star motel with an interior that had the beauty of functionality. He smiled as he saw the menu announce the traditional 'English fare' of roast beef and Yorkshire pudding that he ordered with a pint of draught to wash it down. As he did so he thought of all those restaurants that would have offered him something pretentious with wine or waiters that would have at least winced at his choice of food and drink. Here, in this motel, it was acceptable and Ralph enjoyed the freedom that he had long lost shortly after university life.

The waiter brought him the meal that he enjoyed with some relish together with the stodgy steamed pudding that he had for dessert. After dessert the piano player arrived and started playing uninspired but familiar melodies. The pianist was soon accompanied by electronic backing which got a couple to take to the floor. They appeared to be passing through because they were obvious about enjoying their anonymity, disregarding the other guests who looked on.

The 'lady in red' appeared on cue. In her early forties, a confident manner and also obviously passing through, she walked across the dance floor to the bar. Ralph watched her with a deliberate stare the confidence three beers had provided. He liked her skirt; tight enough for his imagination to cope with as well as her red blouse, which although he felt was a little bright for the combination, provided a lightness and freedom of movement to breasts that still, looked good for her age.

She sat at the bar with the confidence of a 'working girl' and was served with what he guessed was a gin and tonic. The barman affected deliberate courtesy. Ralph wasn't sure whether the barman was well tutored in customer service or whether he was using the disguise of working behind the bar to spend more time fantasizing an encounter with a 'lonely passer through'.

Ralph ordered a drink. He was a little tired, he knew he should try and get some sleep but the pleasure of looking at this lady that obviously, it seemed to him, enjoyed the pleasure of having an audience seemed a more attractive option.

Alison did enjoy an audience. Men provided her with

that something that went beyond the ordinariness of relationships. She enjoyed the power of arousing interest on demand. It was for her a realization that could come only after losing something that promised immortality. She had married young after being swept off her feet by a romance that went beyond an inordinate plethora of adolescent charm and the novelty of sex. Hers had been a life that mirrored the burden of womanhood, the giving up of the dream of being pampered with leisure and children to afford the luxury of a mortgage. The early years were fulfilling through arguments born of not having enough money, of making do with second hand when new things were out of reach and children were an expensive luxury that fuelled ambition and the child allowance, a necessity for the poor.

Fourteen years of saving and childless yearning had ended in the acquisition of a semi-detached house in the suburbs and a divorce. The settlement meted out by the Courts took into account the fact that she had a career but made no allowances for an early abortion followed by years of contraception that deprived her of the years of remaining unfulfilled. The career seemed to be all that was talked about during the divorce hearings. A couple that dreamed of making it and sacrificed what little chance they had of love. As soon as it all came together it was time to move on. It was after a year of the divorce that she realized what was in store for her. Friends that were still couples tried to set her up with someone as if by doing so they would not have to put up with the discomfort of an odd number of guests at dinner parties or at least not have to listen to the constant moaning of someone for whom a relationship had gone sour.

Close to forty, as she had been, she noticed that men for whom she was still an object of scrutiny were married and clichéd in their seduction methods. Alison had been seduced by so many of them that they now seemed immature. At least those that were divorced seemed more honest about having some fun or passing the time with no lies to encourage hope.

She noticed Ralph as she walked into the bar cum restaurant of the motel. She instinctively knew he was married and also that he had noticed her. She noticed the unnecessary drink that he had ordered after the meal. The barman's pathetic attempts to play the gigolo had not gone unnoticed either but she had nothing better to do than sit there and pass the time. It was at least better than sitting in her room watching television. There were a few couples but no one of any interest. The barman was becoming less subtle as the evening wore on and so she made a move. The next time Ralph was looking she caught his gaze and smiled. She knew he would be over in a few minutes and Ralph didn't disappoint her.

Ralph was at first a little embarrassed at being caught out but then remembered the smile. He looked around the room one last time to make sure there wasn't anyone he knew and then walked up to the bar cradling the whisky he had ordered. He took the bar stool, moved it a discreet distance from Alison's and then, exuding confidence, placed his drink on the bar and sat down.

'Hello,' said Ralph with a smile, 'Quiet here isn't it?'

Alison took a long rehearsed sip of her drink to generate excitement. The barman acknowledged the predictability of the situation and came over on cue to ask them whether they would like anything else.

'Another gin and tonic?' asked Ralph as if to impress Alison with his powers of observation or at least in the hope that he was paying Alison a compliment by knowing what she was drinking.

'Sure.'

'And another whisky for me,' said Ralph.

Ralph was not fluent in the language of infidelity but he had learned a lot from observation and, while excursions on business trips had often taken him fairly close there was usually someone he knew either with him or close by who had the moral indignation to draw the line by threatening a public reprimand. It was always a pleasant change to find himself with the freedom to take it a little further than he usually did.

The next morning, waking up to the sound of a shower he was surprised at himself. Although he was proud that he had been able to pull it off he was surprised that he had spent the night; once the conquest was made there seemed little point in risking tenderness. It was nice to wake up to the sound of a shower when the experience had been pleasurable as well as satisfying. The guilt may come later but Ralph didn't see any point in spoiling it now.

Alison walked in with a towel for modesty that the sunlight peering through the windows demanded.

'I am glad you're awake. I think you had better get going before I throw you out.'

Ralph obeyed with a smile. Got dressed and left. There was not much conversation. Most of the conversation had been used up in the foreplay that started in the bar and stopped when conversation was no longer necessary.

Alison had passed an enjoyable night and Ralph had been tender enough for her to allow Ralph to stay the night. That was something she had denied herself as a matter of course. Her entry into the world of single women had taught her this security measure that went hand in hand with the others that the new 'health and safety' rules of casual sex demanded.

'Will I see you tonight?'

'Maybe.'

Ralph kissed her on the cheek.

'It was a great night. You were fantastic.'

Alison didn't believe him but that didn't matter. Compliments were always nice.

No promises to meet up that evening. No plans made and no privacy infringed. Ralph did not think much of it until his return that evening. Late after a business dinner where those under his influence had feted him he returned to the bar. He ordered his second drink before he asked the barman whether Alison had been in that evening and on being told that she had not simply shrugged his shoulders and gazed around at the guests who had nothing better to do than to listen to the bored piano player pouring out 'easy listening' melodies that had long since transformed themselves into background music no one ever listened to anymore.

Ralph was glad in a way that Alison wasn't there. He knew from friendly advice supported by experience that 'twice' encouraged the familiarity that turned one-night stands into affairs. Anyway, he was going home the next day and a night of celibacy would encourage him to put the incident behind him and be more affectionate to Judy when he got home. For the moment it seemed that Joe's diagnosis might not be correct. That certain age had not yet arrived for Ralph.

*   *   *

That is what scorpions do

A friend once told me a joke about a frog and a scorpion. The punch line is 'That is what scorpions do'. I laughed when I heard the joke. I think I laughed because it happened to someone else. I promise to tell you the joke if you read to the end of the story I am about to tell you. You can cheat if you want to. No excuses required.

Frances

I knew Frances long before I met Charles. She was an intelligent young lady in her late twenties on the way to a successful career in the city. I liked her because she allowed me to flirt with her. We men are simple in our pleasures, especially those of us who are married. You will note I call her a lady and not a girl. I am not being politically correct. I am assuming you are a female reader and I don't want to miss an opportunity to flirt with you.

Her hair was shoulder length, brown eyes set in an independent career minded face and figure bordering on the petite all of which I found attractive. She used her sexuality to good effect. I think I had my first imaginary affair with her even before she was properly introduced. Still early into my marriage I was happy to content myself by having imaginary affairs and sharing dirty jokes with friends over a few drinks.

In addition to being attractive Francis was the sort of girl not easily upset by the antics of a group of half drunk colleagues who given half a chance would have slept with her. She gave 'as good as she got'. A feminist in a skirt and nail polish that I think deep down enjoyed being a tease. I enjoyed being part of the group and it was not long before I got the knack of lying.

'Sorry sweetheart, we have a visiting divisional director who needs to be entertained and I drew the short straw. I'll be home as soon as I can. Don't wait up.'

My wife didn't like it at first but after a few rows where I played the part of the injured party working hard to give her the good life I promised her she learned to tolerate the infrequent late evenings when I arrived with the mixed smell of alcohol and breath fresheners. She soon found a group of friends for herself that helped me get over any guilt I may have had in the early days of our marriage.

Francis did quite well and within a short time was offered a secondment to Australia. I was a little envious but then I was sensibly married and those sorts of adventurous career options, even if they existed, were not for the likes of me. Of course Francis was out of my league and when she left I sensibly put the sexual fantasy in the 'bad luck' compartment of the part of the brain marked 'Memories – use with discretion'.

Life was good to me. Shortly after Frances left I met a group of friends and we decided to form a drinking club. A group of like minded pseudo-intellectuals who had decided that in order to put the world to right we would meet in a bar to discuss current affairs, art, culture and, of course, women every Friday evening. Sport was allowed as a topic of discussion only if our patriotism would otherwise be compromised!

There were five of us in the group, a gallery owner, a property developer, a banker, an accountant and Charles, a management consultant. Introductions at a bar to celebrate the impending wedding of a mutual friend led to an exchange of telephone numbers and three weeks, and two meetings later the group was formed. Eleven o'clock was generally our cue to leave as all of us except Charles were married and regular Friday night drinking came with domestic restrictions, which, if ignored, could jeopardise the success of the arrangement.

Charles

Charles had just turned fifty and although balding he was also destined to have gout as a penance for lack of exercise and passion for good cheese and wine. He was a confirmed bachelor and boasted of his good fortune of having fallen in love with himself early on in life and so avoided the emotional and financial destruction that those less fortunate had to live through. His love of himself was second only to a love of Mahler. His collection of great performances was, he said, the most comprehensive he had ever come across. Those of us privileged to have found ourselves in his apartment were envious of his apparent hedonistic delight in the creed of bachelorhood. Good food, good wine and, good company, all in homage to desire, were enviable. There was always a question of how his sexual needs were satisfied. We speculated about the mistress, the prostitutes and depending on the mood we were in whether 'boys' were more his cup of tea. We had never seen him with women and although he could be extremely vulgar when he spoke of women there was enough doubt that his vulgarity could be a 'cover up'.

So that was Charles. Never entertained at home and hated being invited to dinner other than at a restaurant. He apologised for not accepting invitations, which, he explained as the tediousness of eating badly without the right to retaliate. The wives that met him thought he was gay and safe and flirted with him and he in turn obliged although we noted he avoided any physical contact with them.

'A peck on each cheek at fifty yards,' we used to joke, 'Charles, you don't get Aids from a kiss on a cheek!'

The meeting

It was two years later that Frances reappeared on the scene. I remember her having returned from her stint in Australia. Why she had got in touch with me I am still not sure, but she did. It was a Friday too. I wanted very much to meet her, hear what she had been up to and what she was planning to do and still had fond memories of flirting with her. Although it was not generally allowed to invite guests to our Friday events I decided that an exception, especially someone like Frances, might even be welcomed. Frances was only going to be in town until Sunday. The weekend was out of the question since as accommodating as my wife could be there were limits that needed to be observed. That was of course not allowing for my presumption that Frances would have nothing better to do over the weekend, or that I thought introducing her to the group would give me an opportunity to show off.

We were late. Well, the truth is, we had stopped off at a wine bar for a quick drink. I wanted some time with my attractive acquaintance to myself. Although reluctant at first about gate crashing a men only party Frances agreed. I think it was the excitement of being with a group of generally married or middle-aged men that persuaded her. After all I have never met a woman, married or otherwise, who did not like to be the centre of attraction.

I saw Charles's jaw drop when he saw us although he quickly recovered with a remark about my not needing any excuses about being late. I was flattered by the insinuation and didn't respond. I don't think Frances heard the remark otherwise I am sure that she would have said something in reply. Sexist jokes were not something she believed were the prerogative of men only.

I introduced Frances as the equivalent of my boss, which in terms of grade she was and I think Frances enjoyed that deference. I told her not to let that go to her head because we went back a long way (the earlier insinuation reinforced) and I would not allow her any privileges other than those I freely gave. She told me to stop trying to act like a man and we all laughed. It was an easy introduction.

We spent more time chatting that evening than our 'evening out' passes allowed and except for Charles and Frances who were free agents we knew we were in for trouble when we got home. The wine continued to flow, Charles made sure of that, and Frances gave us a diversion that we had not had before. I left at midnight. Frances said she was a big girl and would get a Taxi. She wasn't a big girl but at thirty-three and having back-packed in South America and Australia, I accepted that she was probably better equipped to look after herself than I was. I left Charles, Andrew and Frances at the restaurant finishing off the wine. Having received two calls already from Mary I decided that it was probably not worth pushing my luck and sacrificed my pleasure in staying with them a little longer. Having a wife has its' obligations. Something about 'the better part of valour' comes to mind.

Charles didn't make the next meeting and when he was sheepish at the meeting two weeks later we decided he was up to something. We had never seen Charles appear so unsure of himself and after suffering a few digs he finally became very serious.

'Now shut up the lot of you. I have something I want to tell you.'

We didn't say a word. James sniggered but soon realised that it was out of place and joined us in affected anticipation.

Affectation gave way to an awkward silence.

'Charles, is everything ok?' I asked.

'Look, everything is fine. I like you lot and we have been enjoying our weekly meetings for about a year now haven't we. I have grown rather fond of you and therefore it was a difficult decision to make as to whether to leave you all or alternatively see if we can still be friends.'

This did not sound like Charles at all.

'Charles, you're killing us with the suspense. Will you for God's sake come out with it? What the hell is the problem?'

He told us and after a momentary silence we all burst out laughing. I know we shouldn't have but we did.

'You cannot be serious. Charles getting married! You have got to be kidding. The world must be coming to an end. Fifty years of self-assured security and now the last bastion of bachelorhood bites the dust. Charles you were our only hope.'

The others had stopped laughing before I did and were all staring at me.

'For God's sake can't you stop being so insensitive.'

It was James that shut me up.

After paying our respects to the dead, Harry, patronising as ever, asked the question.

'Alright, Charles, who is she and what happened?'

What came next threw us completely. It was Frances!

I think telling the story you probably guessed it was but none of us had an inkling. Francis was thirty-two and Charles was not handsome.

The marriage

Charles and Francis were married within a month. They didn't have a church wedding and no big reception to follow. The Friday group met at the registry office with our wives and it was a generally subdued affair. Charles and Frances left for a two-week honeymoon in Barbados and we agreed that we would celebrate when they got back.

Our weekly meetings died out shortly after Charles got married. We spoke a few times on the telephone but Charles was clearly on a leash. After a while we stopped trying to get him out. I was surprised that our group didn't manage to stay together after Charles left but I found another group of friends to be with on Friday evenings. Mary had got used to my evenings out with the boys and continuity was necessary to make sure she would continue to accept them.

I heard about Frances from time to time over the next year or so and then, to my delight, got transferred to her division. She was different at work. Treated me like dirt if I stepped out of line but I got the chance to get my own back. The business trips were fun and we had a great time off duty. She was secure in her marriage but made it very clear about being in charge of her own life. There was no sense of urgency in our affair; we merely took advantage of the opportunities as they presented themselves. Another promotion for Frances meant it didn't last long but it certainly was memorable. No need to fantasise any more; memory reclassified.

Charles never rang me and except for the exchange of Christmas cards our friendship lapsed. In the circumstances I didn't really mind.

I occasionally felt sorry for Charles. He was a good sort, harmless and good company. It must have been difficult for him living with someone like Frances but then we all choose the life we live in more respects than we ever like to acknowledge.

Chance encounter

It was a year or so later that I found myself in Harrods. I was planning to go on holiday and needed a new suitcase. Walking down an escalator I noticed a familiar form in a linen suit in front of me. I knew immediately it was Charles. I called out to him as he stepped off the escalator.

'Hello Charles, I thought it was you, how are you? You're looking well? Haven't seen you in years.'

He turned towards me in the tired lumbering manner that was so Charles. He looked a little confused as if he, for a moment, was trying to recognise something familiar but couldn't quite remember exactly what it was.

'Charles, it's me. Don't you remember me, you old bugger.'

His expression changed from one of confusion to pain. He stood there staring at me for a moment. I thought I saw tears well up in his eyes just before he turned and walked away.

That evening I decided to give James a call. We hadn't spoken for months so we had a lot to talk about. He mentioned Charles before I could talk about my chance encounter with him that afternoon.

'Did you hear about Charles?'

'Actually, I saw him this afternoon in Harrods. The bugger didn't recognise me. Can you believe that? What about him?'

'Charles and Frances have split up. Apparently she has been having an affair with someone at work and she has decided to leave him. I understand the poor bugger took it badly.'

Epilogue

There was a frog and a scorpion on the bank of a river. The frog was just about to jump in to swim across when the scorpion asked whether the frog would allow the scorpion to ride piggyback because he too wanted to cross the river.

The frog was not stupid and said no but the scorpion explained that he would not sting the frog because if he did they would both drown and he had no desire to die. The frog thought that was a reasonable explanation and agreed.

Half way across the river he felt the sting of the scorpion. He looked up at the scorpion in disbelief.

'Why?'

The scorpion shrugged his shoulders and said, 'I am a scorpion. That is what scorpions do?'

*   *   *

Cycles

I saw you smile at me and I thought I saw something more. I smiled back wondering whether I was imagining something more than was there as I always did and so treated it as politeness. You smiled again and I did the same and so it continued until I could take no more and I asked you out.

It was an awkward date but then first dates always are. I asked you things and you replied and I tried to read between the lines. I couldn't see the meaning behind the simple words and yet in the unexpected answers I felt that the awkwardness was felt by you too.

Take me now or wait until I get to know you better. Are we going to be friends or is there more to it than that? I was not sure. I wanted to ask you out again. I thought it would be good to wait until the weekend. I could work in the meantime. I could go out with my friends and see you at the weekend. It was nice to wait and see what would happen. Would I sleep with you this weekend or was a second date too soon. I would wait until we met and then over the course of the date read those signs that I thought were standard. The moment when it becomes obvious that something is on offer. Shall I do something? I don't want this to end. If I rush into it too soon I would risk losing the opportunity of future 'innocent' meetings. Never, no matter how much I wanted them to they would never come again. It would be as if a possible experience would have been lost. The experience of waiting for that moment from which there is no turning back. I would not be drawn into making that mistake.

It was Tuesday and still three more days to go. I would only have one day at the weekend because you had indicated that you needed to do the household chores that would get you prepared for the next week. The long routine of the week ahead and so there were maybe four days to go. You had not said which day you would be free this weekend. Oh well, I would wait and see.

I sat watching television that evening but I don't remember what I saw. We had only had one date and therefore I could walk away. A relationship had not yet started. I didn't need to call anything off. There was nothing to call off. The day had ended and it was time to think through the consequences of what future actions could bring.

'Hi, it's me. How are you?'

'Fine.'

'I missed you.'

I didn't mean to say that. Perhaps she didn't hear me. It was too early in the relationship to say that. I was stupid. It's OK. I don't think she heard.

'I missed you too.'

Oh God! That was sweet. Did you hear that? She said she missed me too.

'Are you free at the weekend?'

'Of course, do you want to do something?'

Yes I wanted to do something but I did not know what. It was too early to sleep together. If we did then we really would be starting a relationship and it was too early. We had to be sure. I knew that once we had slept together that would be it. Relationships have a habit of 'fast forward' when that happens.

'Yes, I want to do something.'

I thought long and hard to make what I wanted to do sound interesting so that she would say yes. I mean yes to meeting up.

'What are you doing now?'

I was buying time. It was pointless though because I didn't know what to do. I just wanted to see her but I knew just saying that sounds boring. I think about what she might be thinking about...'what does he mean that he just wants to see me, is that a date. Don't we do anything! He just wants to come over spend some time looking at me and then wants to leave! That sounds perverted. Maybe he's one of those sorts of people that are best avoided. I can't think what they are called and I don't know what they do but I know that they are not normal.'

'Nothing.'

I am on the path to destruction. There is nothing to talk about. I try and ask questions but the responses demand more. I am going away soon and so I have to see her even though we do not have a relationship. I don't want a relationship. I want to be able to walk away at anytime. That way nobody gets hurt. She can walk away too. Anytime. We do not have a relationship.

'We could go for a walk.'

Stupid suggestion. There is nothing exciting about going for a walk. It is so boring. Nothing to do. I will have to make conversation but that doesn't come easily to me. What do I do now? I should have asked her whether she wanted to see a film but I couldn't think of a film that might be good. I should have checked before I phoned. Shall I ask her whether I could ring back? No, that would be silly. Who would ever do that? It would take a while to find out what films were on and then I would have to read the reviews because I couldn't ask her out to see a film if there was nothing interesting on.

'Have a coffee in the park?'

Might as well stay on the slippery slope to failure! If I fail it wouldn't matter because we don't have a relationship.

'OK. When do you want to meet?'

We met at eleven. It was a nice park. I should have picked her up at her place. I don't know why but I suppose I should have. Anyway, it's too late now and it doesn't matter anyway. Meeting at the park is OK. I have often seen girls or guys waiting at the entrance of the park, trying not to look as if they are waiting for someone and ending up looking more obvious than ever.

We walked and talked and laughed. We occasionally got serious until that is I noticed and then changed the subject.

Stupid really, I can't really remember anything. It is one of those wasted days when something wonderful happens and all you can remember is the feeling. I don't know what

I am doing, I can't really pay attention. I am losing the opportunity of having something to think about until next weekend. There is nothing I can think of and it is still only Tuesday evening. What am I going to do for the next three days! Maybe it will be Sunday again which will mean that it will be four days. I really ought to get a hold of myself!

'Hello, it's me.'

'How are you?'

'Fine.'

'It was a lovely day on Sunday.'

'Yes it was.'

Oh God, did you hear what she said. She really liked the walk in the park. I knew she would. Well, almost. It was a nice walk. I want to do it again, but we can't always end up going for walks, can we! It would get boring and then she wouldn't want to see me again and I so much want to see her again.

I am so glad that we are not in a relationship. I didn't sleep with her. It was just a walk. Relationships only start after you have sex, right! I know because I have been through that sort of relationship before. I don't want to sleep with her. I just want to see her more often.

'Pity you live so far away otherwise I would have invited you over for a coffee.'

She might have stayed over. It is Tuesday still and we would both have to go to work the next day. Well, not necessarily. We could call in sick! People do and no one would really notice. I couldn't go in the day after that because it would be too obvious. Would have to plan it on a Thursday so that we could call in sick on Friday and then spend the weekend together and then arguably, having spent the weekend recovering, we could go into work looking well. Not really, because everyone would have thought that we just wanted to have a long weekend and didn't want to use up our holidays.

'Why don't you move closer?'

Now there is an idea! We could then meet often and we wouldn't end up having a relationship. We could accidentally bump into each other and if neither was doing anything we could meet up and do something together. It wouldn't matter even if we were doing something because having met we could agree to meet after we had finished doing whatever we were doing. You see, it's simple really. We wouldn't end up having a relationship and therefore even though we could walk out on each other we would not hurt each other. I would have to make sure that I did not sleep with her. That would be necessary otherwise, well it would be different.

'OK, I'll move closer next weekend.'

I was joking. Do you think I am that crazy? Do you think that I don't know any better?

I told you I was not going to have a relationship.

'The weekend seems a long way away.'

'Who says that we have to wait for the weekend?'

'OK, want to see a film tomorrow.'

'Which one?

You see what I mean. I knew I shouldn't have said that. I don't know why I said it. I just dropped my guard. The thought of a silence was frightening. I just said that for something to say. It didn't matter what we planned to do because all I wanted to do was to be with you but I couldn't say that.

'Do you have anything that you want to see?'

If she did she would have said so wouldn't she, stupid! God! I do ask such stupid questions.

'Don't know really but we could have a chat tomorrow. That will give us each sometime to look up what is playing.'

We agreed a time and saw a film. It wasn't much but luckily she chose. We went back to her place. I mean I took her home. I know I did not need to because it wasn't that late. I told myself that I would not stay because you can never be sure when through some accident a relationship could start and then that would be it.

We would meet more frequently. The sex would be interesting. I would want to see her everyday. She would start making plans. I would want her to move in with me. She would. We would live together and everything would be wonderful, the start of the domestic existence which we would act out with politeness. The politeness would tire us out so much that the sex would either not be something that I could look forward to every day or it would be boring. That would be a relationship. We would get bored and one day one of us would leave. That is why you should not have sex if you want the relationship to last for a long time. I know these things.

'Do you want to come in for a coffee?'

'I would love to but I think you are tired. You have work tomorrow. I'll call you tomorrow.'

I noted sadness in her voice. She wanted me to stay. I know about these things. I had to be strong for both of us.

'Alright, goodnight.'

I kissed her goodnight, on the cheeks and then in parting on her lips too. She did taste sweet. It turned into a long kiss and then, well, what the hell! I went in for coffee!

*   *   *

The Feminist

I

There has been a lot of talk about the battle of the sexes over the centuries. Even when it was generally understood that one lived in either a patriarchal or matriarchal society there still seemed to be a general recognition that men were the stronger of the sexes and therefore were expected to dominate in any relationship. I have always thought of the female of the species to be the weaker of the sexes and in that belief have always deferred to them as by definition they require special consideration. It was in this mood that I proudly supported feminists of the liberation age skipping over the issue of abortion with a mental agility that only youth affords.

That was of course a long time ago and although I retained an affected reverence for women generally it is true to say that with age I pigeon holed them depending on the relationships they embodied such a mother, sister, daughter or wife. I never thought of the lover as being anything other than someone men were allowed to fantasise about but who could not exist because the consequences were too frightening to imagine. Such was the lower middle class background that I was brought up in. Destined to grow up as all youth is reminded to do I too grew up relying on friends on whom I could test my theories and the absence of a family left me little to resent.

Colin was part of my growing up. A tall, slim man who I had known as one of my surrogate fathers that came with a very fortunate placement strategy that was in those days unmarred by the extra self destructing criteria that adoption agencies have developed to ensure that children remain in children homes for as long as possible. My foster parents were all kind and, whether it was for the money or the love of having children to call their own, they all earned my love and gratitude. I found nothing confusing about growing up in a home of mixed faiths, ethnic backgrounds or cultural variety unless having a liberal mind is a handicap, but then that is something that text book sociologists are always going find a life time's work funded by a government that needs to be seen to be making the right noises.

Colin and Mary, his wife, were white. Both in their forties with no children of their own. A couple that had fallen in love in the sixties and who had matured out of 'hippihood' by finding that a stable profession and a semi-detached house in the suburbs was not as bad as all they were made out to be. That was particularly true when their education and background gave them a choice of not having to live on unemployment benefit in a Council flat if they didn't want to.

Their shock came later on when after years of contraception they found out that had all been a waste of time, as Mary could not conceive. After the initial coming to terms with the fact that they could not have children they both decided that it was not as bad as it seemed because they could always adopt. It was during their discovery of childless parenthood that they stumbled across fostering and decided to take that up instead of adoption for the fun of a variety of children that they could in theory get rid of if they didn't like them. Cynically, I am sure that the money offered for fostering figured in the decision making process.

That is how I appeared on the scene, all of fourteen years old and with an immediate crush on Mary. Shown to my room I was allowed to unpack and join them in the sitting room for a chat. My helper went down to meet them to start the patronising lecture that she had perfected and which I had heard many times before.

Colin was the quiet one. He always let Mary have her way. I was never sure why he seemed to have no interest in standing up for himself but, I suppose, if you saw Mary you would understand that he was well compensated.

My stay with them lasted me up to finishing school. The stability of two years enabled me to go on to study for my A levels and then by a stroke of good fortune I got into a minor university which gave me the feeling of achieving something that my background would not normally have allowed.

My mostly unsuccessful affairs in my first two years of university left me without a mate that everyone else seemed to have found and being used as a fop, while being useful for recreation purposes, left me one of the odd ones at parties.

It was in my third year that I found someone who I thought might be right for me. A feminist in the traditional mode – braless and sexless, Vikki was a huntress. She used me for fun to begin with but having made the right noises she decided to keep me as her own. Her belief in complete emancipation without regard to traditions, religion or marriage allowed me to enjoy serving her well. It was nearly six months after we met that the word love was first mentioned. I had decided that the word would be an anathema to her and had refrained from using it so when Vikki, with her smeared black lipstick and eyes of a five year old, asked me whether I loved her I hedged my bets by faking momentary deafness. I don't think she believed it because she didn't repeat the question.

A month later it was repeated as a statement.

'I love you Jam.'

Jam was a nickname given to me because the English find it hard to pronounce the name given to me by my mother before I was given up for adoption. Why she had chosen the name Jamshed had always been a mystery to me. It was an Indian name but I was a half cast, half Indian and half West Indian. The irony was that it was meant to be a Muslim name too.

'Do you Vik?'

'Yea, you're fucking great!'

I wasn't sure whether the reference was to my sexual prowess or embarrassment at the show of female emotion that caused the manner in which the affirmation was given but, to be honest, I didn't care. I loved her and she loved me too.

II

We lived together after university. Vikki's hair changed colour and her clothes became more acceptable to employers. Having spent six months on the dole was long enough to realise that freedom had its' limitations.

Vikki joined the social services and enjoyed her work in a hostel for battered wives. I joined a local authority in a department where I was one of the few with a university education. Soon promoted to run a department of ethnic equal opportunity refugees I saw the irony of being placed with my own people.

Vikki lectured me most evenings on the evils of men and I of course agreed. Not always because I found it expedient to do so but also on occasion because I believed the accusation to be valid. The stories she came out with of inmates at the hostel were extraordinary with domestic rape taking a low ranking in the horror stakes. I reinforced my views on the rights of women and the responsibility of society to safeguard women from the effects of economic slavery and never forced Vikki to have sex with me if she didn't want to.

I helped Vikki out at weekends when being a man was not a hindrance. I enjoyed doing something useful as well as being with Vikki at the same time. If we were married it would have been a successful marriage that had lasted for over three years.

But life is not quite that straight forward. The moral dilemmas are easy to ignore when creature comforts are more or less freely available. Neither of us wanted children and we had always been careful to ensure that we didn't have any, no matter how passionate the inspiration might be.

How Vikki became pregnant I will never know.

The first week she was late with her periods we put it down to tension caused by stress at work. Too frightened to get a do-it-yourself pregnancy test from the chemist meant that it was three weeks before Vikki decided to go and see the doctor. I wanted to go with her but she didn't want me too. Of course being a girl she didn't come out and say so.

'It's OK, Jam. I can go myself. There is no need for you to take time off work. I said it is ok. I don't need my hand held. Jam, will you get off my fucking back! I said I don't want you coming with me.'

I took the hint. She was only three weeks late and that is too soon for complications, isn't it?

I didn't go. I was guilty about what I had done to her. I always made sure we were safe, even when we did drugs at university.

She didn't say much after she found out. I tried to speak to her but she told me to piss off so I left her alone with a passing shot that I would support her, whatever her decision.

That night was the first time I had ever seen her cry. I didn't know what to do. She told me to leave her alone so I sat on the side of the bed until she screamed at me to fuck off. I went into the only other room we had in our council flat and sat there listening to her cry. I couldn't help it. My tears fell because I didn't know what was happening. I didn't know for sure why Vikki was so upset. I tried to explain it away by the fear of giving birth, the loss of her independence, betrayal of a way of life that she had chosen, perhaps even the thought that she may end up like one of those women that she looked after in the hostel. Without Vikki's help I didn't know the answer. I thought confirming to her that I would stand by her would be enough.

Vikki left me a week later. I tried to find her but couldn't. She didn't turn up for work. I went to the police to try and trace her but they wouldn't help me. It was a domestic case and if my girlfriend didn't want to see me, an assumption they felt justified in making without talking to her, that was her right. What was worse was that they cautioned me that if I tried to trace her they might have to intervene on the basis of harassment. It was strange to find myself in such a situation.

I didn't hate Vikki for leaving me. I wanted to apologise for making her pregnant. I wanted to let her know that I respected her rights as a woman and accepted my guilt as a man but those thoughts did not last for long. I decided that it was too difficult trying to be a male feminist and found a traditional sort of life with someone who wanted marriage, a mortgage and children. The marriage and mortgage were easy, the children a problem. The doctors diagnosed a rare male infertility condition, which meant that I was useless as a man. They could not determine when this condition had first arisen and in those days artificial insemination was not a financial option. The social services were as helpful as they usually are and could not approve our receiving a grant.

Sue didn't leave me although I expected her to. I even suggested that I would understand if she did which was not a sentiment that she appreciated. We decided to adopt and when we found that mixed race couples with no religious heritage were only eligible to adopt handicapped children we decided to foster. It seems it is easier to get paid well for looking after children temporarily than it is to take a child for life. I am not complaining. After all it's good fun. Sue likes it better than having to work.

*   *   *

The Party

I don't really like promotion parties. They are all very much the same. Meeting people that you have successfully avoided outside such events, making new promises of everlasting friendship coupled with well laid plans to leave before the increasing consumption of free alcohol reduces one's conversation to a noticeable slur. The opportunity to meet new people is welcome for the first few invitations that accompany success but then they degenerate into events one attends out of necessity. The need is well articulated by agents and depleting bank accounts that have become a sieve for droplets of the blood of mammon. Boring people with money or power and their sops all gather round to patronise with well-worn epithets and the occasional offer of casual half-drunken sex or better still, drugs. Of course I generalise but if one bad apple were enough I feel justified when experience shows most of them to be bad.

I suppose that is what I do now, attend parties because I have to. My success no longer requires scratching around for parties to promote myself and therefore I accept only those invitations that my agent gets desperate about. I know I am ungrateful for what I have achieved but then I think that is a malaise that all human beings suffer albeit some more than others. I do my bit for world peace and the alleviation of poverty by freely giving my name to Amnesty International and Christian aid. Unfortunately I cannot redeem myself in terms of relationships though with three divorces to my name and twice as many children I have shared my financial success. My publisher and agent often warn me of the perils of writers block induced by excessive alcohol and drugs but endowed with an ability to write saleable fiction, despite being semi-conscious, has helped me avoid humility in the face of what is clearly sound advice.

Meeting Clare at one of those parties and the one night stand that followed was not noteworthy at the time. It was only some four months later that I was reminded of the incident and that was at another party. A poor girl that life had dealt a terrible blow to and from which only the most stubborn recover. It took me a while to recall her and if it wasn't for the tenacity that Freddy showed when he had nothing better to do I would have let it pass without any thought. In the end I gave him a 'Oh yes, I remember. What a shame,' and accepted his rebuke of being a 'Heartless bastard,' with indifference. It was on the way home, half drunk as usual, that I recalled her.

Clare was the last girl at the party who had not been taken. Slightly tall for the company of men at the party she had been left for those who had not made a move early on or who were too drunk to care. I remember numerous messages on the answer phone after the event as if I had a heart or conscience or I really cared about the watch I had left behind.

Clare had taken an overdose. Nothing, I hasten to add, anything to do with me. Freddy of course had no interest in her other than the recollection that we had left together. I only had a vague recollection of getting home the next day and had regretted forgetting my watch at her place only because it might mean that I would need to sleep with her again. Clare gave up trying to meet me and returned the watch by courier. It was a cheap Rolex that I had written off having set my heart on a new one. I could of course afford to buy a new one but the watch had been a present from the only woman to leave me that I cared about and having two was the same as throwing one away. Ridiculous as that may sound I promise you it's true. Having left it at Clare's was perfect. I could now say that I had lost it or that it had been taken as a penalty for unsatisfactory sex.

I didn't know Clare did drugs and the fact that she had managed to take a lethal overdose was evidence enough that she was no professional. Obviously, she hadn't been doing drugs for long. I felt sorry for her enough to ditch the easy lay that I had managed to pick up at the party.

I rang Freddy the next day to say I was sorry. Freddy didn't know what I was talking about. I reminded him and he called me a little shit, which made me feel better. It is somehow cleansing to receive admonishment for one's misdemeanours, like receiving a penance of Hail Mary after confession.

Freddy was a good friend who I had known for over twenty years. He had helped me get an agent that was not embarrassed about pushing my work and had read one of the early drafts of my first novel. He was the one who had helped me discipline myself to the one thousand words that I continue to write every day. He was also the friend who I no longer met because he was of no use to me. He had given up drinking and drugs thanks to Judy, his now wife, who had put him through a program of sex for rehabilitation. We had nothing very much in common after I had made a drunken pass at Judy, unsuccessfully I might add, and Judy, who never liked me, told him. He told me he didn't believe Judy and made an excuse by saying that she had probably said it because she thought I was a bad influence. Freddy, sober and lecherous, did talk to me each time we met in public when Judy was not around to chaperone.

I wrote a short story about my one night stand with Clare and sent it to some Woman's magazine that published it. My agent was furious that I had not given it to him to place and would have taken me off his books if I had not been a sure bet for a decent earnings base. Freddy didn't know anything about the story otherwise I think he might have called me more than a little shit.

I told Jo about the incident. Jo was the latest friend I had made and with whom I was at risk of entering into a semi-permanent relationship of convenience. I didn't have any secrets from her. There was no reason to have any secrets from someone who was in no way special either in bed or out of it. She was a friend while I had nothing better to do and pleasantly was no floozy with disguised expectation. I told her about the one night stand and then, a few days after I found out, told her about the overdose. The fact that she had not met Clare made it easy for her. She thought it was all right to use Clare for the short story. It helped too that she had not read the short story either. Jo left me for other reasons. An extra marital affair with Freddy appeared to be more satisfying than moving in with me but we agreed to be grown up about it and still be friends. We occasionally ended up in bed together but not through any feeling for each other. Being slightly drunk and in the same place at the same time usually resulted in sleeping together no matter how unmemorable it was going to be.

As time passed Clare increasingly came into my thoughts. I started to feel sorry for her. I started to wish I remembered more of our brief relationship. I started dreaming about her. I didn't have much to do last Sunday and so rang Freddy to ask if we could meet for a drink. He said he was busy. I didn't bother ringing Jo. The Clare thing got bad so I decided to go round to Freddy's anyway. I knew Judy would be a bitch but I needed to speak to Freddy.

Judy was home. She told me Freddy was out. I asked if I could wait for him. She agreed, as I knew she would. People have difficulty in throwing out unwanted guests and I have often taken advantage of that. Just my turning up at the door, what chance did she have? It would have been different if I had rung.

I didn't make another pass at Judy. I wasn't in the mood and to be honest, even if I was, I am not that much of a fool. There are limits to the risks that even I would take and anyway you don't do that sort of thing with someone you know when there is little chance of success.

Judy left me in the sitting room of the tasteless detached house that Freddy was so proud of. I tried to watch television and found its' drone to allow me to fall half asleep. Judy came in an hour later and asked me whether I would like another drink. She didn't like me and that was what I needed. I needed to be purged by the hell, fire and damnation of a priest or an enemy. Both would have been able to do the job. I thanked her for the offer and asked for another whisky. I was pleased that she poured one for herself too. Perhaps she was mellowing?

'You look like shit.'

'Thanks'

'Tired of drink and debauchery or just taking a night off?'

I told her about Clare and she must have detected some remorse in my telling of the story that prevented her from repeating her husband's description of me. She called me irresponsible and told me it was high time that I grew up. I secretly felt sorry for her. I always feel sorry for the self-righteous amongst us. I feel sorry that they believe in the illusion of a life that can never exist but accepted her criticisms. As her lecture continued she turned to the most helpless of womanly attributes. The mother in her welled up in those dry breasts and she gave me a pat on the back on the way for a refill. I understood what she meant. It was the mother that loved me despite the fact that I had consumed her life, the pity that men are able to inspire in women!

I knew I had lost it. She had re-entered her little world of decency and guilt and remorse and I didn't have the energy to explain that she was missing the point. I didn't feel remorse. I hadn't done anything wrong. I hadn't used Clare any more than she wanted to be used. The same way that Judy wanted me to use her that evening.

I left before Freddy got home that night. I dreamt of Clare again. This time we made love and I enjoyed it enough to miss her the next morning. I was sad that she was no longer with us. I wondered whether she had found anyone who cared about her before she had died although I suppose the overdose suggests she hadn't.

It is nice having people care about you. I pawned the Rolex later that day. It is nice to have met people who care about you but it is not nice to be reminded about having lost them.

*   *   *

Someone else

There is a generally held belief that infidelity occurs when there is something missing in a relationship. The search for something better than what fate appears to have dished up and never, during the process, admitting that one had anything to do in making the choices that got us this far. I have found this a rather extraordinary trait in human beings when dealing with the breakdown of a commitment whether that commitment takes the form of a marriage or more modern arrangements agreed upon between two people. I do not mean to be disparaging of human beings as I still claim to be one myself but, like most people, I too find it easier to comment on the inadequacies of others rather than accept self criticism.

Returning to the original thought I also believe that an act of infidelity also needs a protagonist; someone who is not prepared to accept his or her lot in life, someone with the belief that it should be possible to realise the dream that is cultured in us throughout our childhood and into adolescence.

I knew it then as I do now, that there must be something missing and a protagonist for infidelity to happen. One without the other simply translates into the existence of normal relationships experienced by the majority of happy families. This is something I believed was true throughout the thirty-six years before I met Sebastian during which I lived as others do not knowing any better. Simply accepting that what you have is as good as it gets.

A lot younger than I, and with a lot more promise, Seb was someone special and with the potential of becoming one of the beautiful people in this world. In addition to a promising career he had a wife that seemed to be the sort of devoted servant that men usually are reluctant to complain too loudly about not having found, a larger house than he grew up in and family and friends that were happy to applaud his achievements.

I met Seb on holiday. I had just finished a rather gruelling stint without a break and had decided to take a weekend break at a coastal holiday resort that offered nothing except the pleasure of being far away from anything that could remotely cause any excitement. They too had decided to have a weekend break for no other reason than something different to do.

I, not one for waking up late, had tried especially hard that morning to be late for breakfast having suffered the previous day with the unfortunate John and Cecily who had decided to adopted me. Determined that I should relax, they were going to make sure I did and decided on an agenda for the day mapped out as closely as my secretary had the knack of organising my life. You can imagine how tired that made me and how often I wished I was back in the office.

The next day had found me dreading to meet up with them again and I was relieved to find myself alone at breakfast apart from a couple sitting at the far end of the dining room. I nodded a good morning and sat at a table as far away from them as possible. Enjoying my breakfast in silence I was soon lost in thought so much so that I didn't notice them leave.

Later that day I went for a stroll on the beach. It was a pleasant day, the sun shone through the clouds which meant that it was not too hot and the sea was a calm grey-blue gently rushing up the sandy beach and withdrawing in disappointment at not having been noticed. There was a fresh sea breeze blowing the smell of sea salt across my face. I laughed at the thought of using the fact as a source of a new advertising campaign. I wondered what my boss who had chosen the resort herself would say if I signed up a new advertising contract with the local authority while I was meant to be having a break to prevent an incumbent excuse of nervous exhaustion.

Having found a spot calculated to keep me dry for at least a couple of hours from the incoming tide I sat down to watch the sea with no purpose other than I had nothing better to do.

'Hello, enjoying the view?'

I turned around to see Seb and his wife walking past me towards the hotel. They were good looking, tanned such that they could pass for having just returned from the Caribbean and so comfortably in love that Seb hardly seemed to acknowledge his wife.

I acknowledged them and silently thanked them for not joining me but some acquaintances are there to be made whether one likes to or not and this turned out to be one of those.

I had decided not to have dinner at the hotel and had asked the concierge for some ideas on restaurants within a ten-minute walk from the hotel. He gave me a choice of two that he recommended and after declining his offer to make a reservation on the basis that it should not be necessary I set out to find them.

The first one I came to had a noisy bar like atmosphere which was not the sort I was in the mood for and so I decided to find the second. When I saw it at a distance I was already sure that was where I would, if possible, dine. A small Italian restaurant, dimly lit, with music quietly playing in the background I waited for a waiter to notice me. Eventually, with an affected smile that aped a clichéd scene from a bad film, one slid up to me. Well-greased hair, a white shirt, waistcoat and clip on bow tie he asked me, in a thick affected Italian accent, whether I had a reservation.

His smugness increased ten-fold when I apologised for having been so stupid as to have come along without one and I was not sure who was having more fun; me, who didn't really care whether I did dine there that evening or the waiter who was pleased at having the opportunity of belittling a customer for having the arrogance of coming along to the restaurant where he worked without a reservation.

'I am sorry Sir, you see,' he said with a full wave of his arm across the restaurant, 'we are fully booked. Perhaps Sir would like to book a table for tomorrow night?'

'Thank you,' I said, 'but you see I am leaving tomorrow. Never mind, it was silly of me to think that you might be able to squeeze a single diner in somehow.'

His satisfaction grew. I thought I would egg it on a bit more when Seb intervened and spoiled the fun.

'Hello again, fancy seeing you here.'

To both my dissatisfaction and the obvious disgruntlement of the waiter Seb insisted that I join him at his table. I declined but Seb, who decided that he was going to be my saviour, wouldn't take no for an answer. That is how we met for the second time and what then became the start of our friendship.

Helen, his wife, was charming. I apologised for breaking up what appeared to be a romantic dinner. Seb gave her a pat on the shoulder. 'No, we don't mind. You know we've been married for over six years and we don't have to have a romantic dinner to get into the mood, do we darling?' Helen smiled at him as if the remark was one of a type that she had got used to.

We had a pleasant dinner and in an attempt to overcome the embarrassment caused by Seb refusing to allow me to pay for dinner I offered to buy them a night cap back at the hotel.

Seb was clearly the dominant partner. Helen, his support, laughed at his jokes, showed an exaggerated interest in what he was saying and gave the impression that everything she did was genuine. Of course being the cynic I didn't believe it but then my experience had shown that honesty of emotion is not the only road to happiness. They were a happy couple. Matched perfectly, each was happy at the compromise that they had made in life.

We talked, laughed and the evening, though not as I had planned, turned out to be very pleasant. After dessert and more wine we decided to leave the almost empty restaurant to walk back to the hotel. It was a pleasant evening, a welcome coolness after the heat of the day. We were all a little drunk and I enjoyed the pleasure of finding a lot to laugh at. Helen was tipsy too slipping on the artificial cobble stone walk way to the hotel. Seb was walking ahead and it was lucky that I was close by and stopped her from falling. Marriage is a funny business. After all the games that are played to win the partner with whom you plan to spend the rest of your life the enthusiasm peters out. Indifference creeps in with a resolve as deadly as the silence of a snake. It is strange, having spent all that energy, one seems to give up without realising that choices are made and the consequences of change are as traumatic as death and rebirth.

We got to the hotel and, as agreed, decided to go into the bar for a nightcap. Not that we needed one. Helen could hardly walk without an arm to hold on to and Seb decided that she needed to be put to bed. I was surprised that not even the alcohol had made her bold enough to refuse.

'I'll be back in a minute. You wait for me,' he said as he staggered off with Helen. Her awkwardness revealed how close fitting her evening dress was, lilac with a deep plunge back and a plastic see through strap that seemed to bite into her flesh. I wondered why he would want to come back for a drink. I put it down to the fact that her drunken state promised nothing more than the boring snoring of restless sleep which would do nothing to help the night promise a memorable end to the evening.

Looking around the bar there were few guests left awake. The piano player had long been playing to himself and the boredom of those awake hardly encouraged him to play with any desire to entertain.

Seb reappeared no more than 'the few minutes later' he had promised.

'Well, Helen's done for the night.' He said with a wink that suggested the relish of a momentary freedom gained in marriage. 'Her snoring will be driving the other hotel guests to distraction. That's what married women are famous for you know,' he said, 'and of course the predictable orgasm that comes without any sense of adventure.' He added staring into the drink in front of him.

'You never said, have you been married?' he asked as if

suddenly noticing that I was standing there and he didn't have to talk to himself.

'No, somehow relationships never transformed into marriage.'

'Lucky you.'

Life is full of the strangest paradoxes. Those that are not married crave the permanence of the promise marriage has to offer and those that are married, ridicule the institution.

I had always liked the idea of marriage but had never found anyone to take the plunge with. The earnestness of starting a relationship had never appealed to me and the casualness with which I fell into some of my relationships somehow never inspired longevity. No regrets though as it had given me the opportunity to succeed in my career more than I probably would have done otherwise. The relationship with my boss might have played a little part in it but only because she broke it off and I, to be honest, had been relieved. Those types of affairs carry more risk than is necessary to take.

We ordered another. Seb, was definitely the playboy type. Handsome enough, I imagined to be able to inspire any women to live out her fantasy; married or single. His hair was combed back and kept in place with gel, his shirt buttons opened to reveal a bronzed body and a style that projected a life of easy living. I smiled to myself thinking about all the women that he had either had or left disappointed. I imagined how lucky Helen must have felt with her catch, how jealous her girlfriends would have been at their marriage, and how delighted she still seemed to be despite the way he ignored her. Of course I was not sure that he did ignore her because we often judge the happiness of married couples and equally often I suspect get it wrong.

'No much action here.' He said looking around the bar. 'This is a dead place unless they all left early to have a screw!' He laughed at his crudeness. I smiled.

'No, come on, tell me why you never got hitched.'

'I don't know Seb, maybe never found the right person.'

'Aw, don't give me all that shit! If you are not a virgin you will know that they are all the same. That goes for both the moaning in bed and the moaning when they are not!' He laughed out loud enough for the few remaining hotel guests to look up. I laughed too. The whisky was working.

'Why not? You can tell me. We will probably never meet again and I won't tell a soul. You gay?'

I laughed.

'What makes you say that? Do I look gay?'

I noticed the barman smile too, eavesdropping in on our conversation.

Seb moved over and put his arm over my shoulder as if to whisper something to me and instead of saying anything burst out laughing in my face.

I turned away from the foul breath of stale alcohol with the excuse to take a sip of my drink.

Seb was in hysterics. He laughed so hard he almost fell off the half of the bar stool that still offered him some refuge.

I realised that the end of the evening had arrived. Seb would not be able to have much more of a conversation. I said good night and despite Seb's protests went to my room.

The next morning as I was checking out I was handed an envelope. It was a note written almost illegibly.

'Give me a ring when you get back to London. My office number is XXX. Just ask for me. Seb Aldridge'

I would have thrown it away had the Hotel attendant not put the note in the same envelope as my bill. I did not notice it again until I was in my office and my secretary returned it to me as something she had found in the envelope I had given her to prepare my expense claim. I don't know why I didn't throw it away but put it in my drawer with all the other pieces of paper that had escaped the wastepaper basket on earlier occasions.

II

It was about a year later that on a clear out of my desk I came across the note and dialled the number. The operator put me through.

'Hello, Seb Aldridge.'

'Hello Seb, I don't know whether you remember me. We met...'

'Hello, I remember you. You are the lucky bastard who never married. How are you? You certainly took a long time to get in touch. Gary, wasn't it?'

'You've got a good memory.'

'Well, comes with the job. Where are you? Fancy meeting up for a drink?'

It was at that moment I was brought back to the reality of what I had done. I had let curiosity get the better of me and here again, story of my life, I was stuck in a situation that I hadn't thought through. I hadn't imagined that it would end up in meeting up for a drink and yet if anyone had asked me what I had expected to be the outcome of making the call I would have looked stupid if I had said that I didn't think it would end up in a meeting.

We met at a bar just off Soho Square which was a few minutes from our offices in Wardour Street. It wasn't far for Seb to come. It was a Thursday night and although I had planned for that to be one of those evenings when I did nothing in anticipation of a hectic weekend I thought a quick drink would do no harm.

Seb was late. Not by much but late enough to be noticeable. The usual excuses about not being able to get out of the office on time and blaming the traffic passed as idle chat while we both thought of something to say.

'How's Helen?'

'We split up. I just couldn't handle the boredom. She is better off that way.'

I reaffirmed to myself at how predictable people were; desperately in love one minute and bored the next. I had thankfully never had to experience it first hand but with so many examples around me I didn't need to. People around me showed me that side of life with the boredom of repetition.

Seb didn't want to talk about it but, not I suspected because it hurt him to remember Helen, more because as a topic of conversation there seemed nothing interesting to say.

After a couple of drinks we decided to have dinner. I had to eat anyway and the company was good. Seb made me laugh. He seemed to have a wonderful way of laughing at his own jokes which would have been hugely irritating if it hadn't been for the delight that he shared in remembering them.

We found an unpretentious Chinese restaurant where the waiters scowled and the food was served with speed and a lot of shouting in a language that seemed to me to have been born out of that habit. Short sharp bursts of phases that sounded as if they were exclamations and not communication. Sadly, now with the boom and bust that London has faced over the last twenty years those places are no more. If still Chinese they have been replaced by refurbished 'authentic' mass produced Chinese exports of replica museum pieces accompanied by wine cellars that are essential if a restaurant is to succeed.

Having eaten, the bill was set down in front of us with a flourish by which the waiter made it clear that he wanted it paid and the table cleared for the next starving guests that had to eat to absorb the alcohol so that they could get home without incident.

We said our good-byes. Seb took my number and we promised to keep in touch.

III

It took four or five dates before we became lovers and three months or so before he moved in with me. That was over twenty years ago.

I had lived for thirty-six years before I had met someone with whom I had decided to live my dream. Seb chose the life because he was looking for excitement and both of us having found what we were looking for have stuck together. We have a dog and a house in Kew. Seb has the Boxster and I the 911 and we both laugh about the fact that we were both confirmed heterosexuals until we met each other. We were lucky! We had both the something missing and the protagonist!

*   *   *

Friends

I

It was a long time since I had seen her last, fifteen or twenty years at least. Actually I do remember it was eighteen since we decided to have a break after five years of being together. I never thought for a moment that it would not end but when it came it was sudden. It wasn't a death but a trial that lasted a fortnight and then the verdict. Like a Paul Simon song that started with the telling of a tale the ending of which was given away by the melody. A sad, long, yearning that echoed the voice of a singer who if he hadn't written the lyrics was a good actor, someone who could imitate the feelings of another man and left one believing that he knew what it was to have loved and lost.

I hadn't lost though because here I was as agreed, a few years later, in her city. 'If you don't find what you are looking for will you come and find me?' I promised and now outside her apartment building I felt the flutter of wings of a bird that had just landed, my feet firmly on the ground with no risk of falling uncontrollably out of the sky. A hard landing but still I had arrived. I was an optimist again. Everything had the promise of turning up roses. Joan had left me and now I wondered whether Sarah would remember. Grasping at straws as I was.

II

It hadn't been hard to find her. Although she had let her flat her tenants were happy to give me her address. I was surprised that they did not have her telephone number but then she was like that. She was strange in her eccentricities. I didn't entirely believe her tenants but a beggar doesn't have much choice. He doesn't get far arguing that he doesn't believe his target doesn't have any money, best to move on and search for another. I had an address. I did not know where it was but then it wouldn't be difficult to find. I thought like a tourist in an unfamiliar town. I had paid to be here both in cash and preparation in mind and body. The difficulties had been taken for pleasure and I was now having the difficulties associated with taking the pleasures of the tourist.

I went back to the hotel. My room was comfortable but lonely. The apprehension I had felt leaving it in the morning, the tension of the journey back in time had taken their toll. I was tired. I wasn't in the mood to search further that day. I needed a break. I fell out of my clothes and fell into bed and into a sleep that was much needed. The dream was associated with my travels. I remembered her along way away, far in the distance of my memory, in a park that appeared out of nowhere. It was hot and looking for an ice cream vendor I found myself with an ice cream but this time walking with her. She was as I remembered her; a slim dark figure with eyes that cared little for anything far away. Her hair, as usual, tied in a ponytail bounced along.

'Why did you come?'

'I wanted to see you.'

'Did you get married?'

'Yes, and divorced too.'

She smiled as if it was the answer she expected. It was not a smile that made her attractive but definitely one that made me feel inadequate. It was as if all the certainty I had in life had been an illusion. Nothing was ever to come out of it even though I felt so in control of my destiny.

'I am not glad you came. I think of you often but not with pleasure. My life with you was a waste of precious time. I could have done something had you not stolen those years, those important years when I could have done something for myself.'

'I am sorry,' I said.

She walked off. I couldn't follow her. My feet, lead heavy, wouldn't move. I called but she didn't turn to look around. I felt the tears fall and woke up crying.

I was mad to have made the journey. I knew why I had done it. It was partly because I had nothing to do. I had recently lost my job and finding oneself over forty does not make it easy. I had tried for about six soul destroying months and then sitting in the small two roomed flat that was all I had left since the divorce, assessing all that had happened in the forty-eight years of my life, I had stopped at the memory of the lover that delighted me for five years. The one that I had let go because I didn't know how to keep her.

I lay there looking at the ceiling of the hotel room. What a fool. I wished I was dead but then death never comes when you want it. It is like children born to those who don't really want them or those who don't want to die get cancer.

I was here because I had nothing else to do. I thought it might be fun to find her. I got up one morning, looked through old, damp papers from the past for an address or telephone number and then not finding anything got in the car and started the journey. I could afford to waste two weeks in a cheap hotel or bed and breakfast and most important of all I would have something to do. I had tired of the routine of reading the newspaper, watching morning television, and ringing the various agencies trying to convince them that I was not over qualified for the jobs on offer. I tried to convince them that my age was not a problem because I was fit, didn't smoke (I lied), and still had a lot of energy. I tried to think of everything. I told them I would be happy taking orders from someone younger than me and that I had not lost my job because I was not good, simply because I was part of a cost cutting exercise. Nothing seemed to be working and six months is a long time for things not to work.

III

The next day I left the hotel with instructions from the concierge. I had lived here for five years and knew the place but still needed instructions.

It was melodramatic but then the theatre and cinema influence us. That 'willing suspension of disbelief' seemed something I wanted to translate into real life. I felt the feelings of an actor ready to tackle 'Hamlet' and this time do something original. The delusion almost seems to be necessary to avoid thinking about the uselessness of it all.

I found the block of flats. She was staying with her sister. I had never been to her sister's flat. I was in the middle of a large council estate where budding pop artists left their mark on walls built especially for that purpose. I could see the block a five minute walk away. I walked across the square and then suddenly changed my mind. I needed to sit down and have a smoke. There were some climbing frames in the corner with benches around it. Although a weekday and mid-morning there were children playing. A group of young mothers were helping their children on the swings. I wondered why but then assumed it must be half term or something. I walked across and sat on a bench.

I pulled out a pack of cigarettes and lit one. The noise of the children playing was strangely soothing in its distraction. They were enjoying themselves and I smiled. Perhaps that is what I did wrong. I should have had children. Joan had wanted children at first but then as we grew used to the freedom she learned to replace the excuses with an unashamed denial of the need for children. We divorced two years ago and in that time a change had come over her. She was younger than I was. Thirty-nine when she left me, a mother by the time the divorce came through and now very happy living in our house with her partner and two lovely children. I had thought that the freedom from the responsibility of children was what she enjoyed. Although perhaps now thinking about it, not in love but comfortable, I had fallen into the routine of married life, eating out once a week and holidays in the sun which were a riot of indulgence.

When she left me it was a surprise as I am sure it always is. It was hard for her. She had known her current partner off and on for a number of years and I never found out what made the last reunion so different from the others. Perhaps he was the one who rekindled the maternal feelings that I had been able to distract her from. Strange because I always thought that it was dangerous to have children over forty. It seems that is another of those 'old wives tales' that we plan our lives around.

I liked Joan. I liked her a lot. She gave me the sense of belonging that I had always wanted. She was the first to leave me. I had managed to keep the privilege of deciding when I tired of relationships and although difficult I found through practice that it was not hard to leave a lover. In fact they helped end relationships and all I had to do was to allow them the privilege. Sarah was the one I still remembered.

I missed Joan. After she left me my world started to crumble. Our new head of department was appointed once the divorce came through. The company had not been doing very well in recent years and he had been brought in to get the company into shape. When I was called in I had asked whether I could stay on at a reduced salary but that was not an option. I was given some extra money to leave quietly and did. I don't blame him because he had to do what he did. I needed the money but more than the money I needed something to do. I was too old to start again. I had been married for nine years. I was getting older. It was only with Joan that I was comfortable with the process of aging. And here I was, sitting in a children's playground in a foreign town where I had a long time ago lived a dream. Eighteen years had not been long enough to drown the sense of the familiar. I was thirty again and going places.

Sarah had been a challenge at first. She was a quiet, shy girl who did not give in easily. to colloquialisms. Conscious of the way she looked but confident that she was worth looking at. She took a long time getting to know. I suppose the fact that she appeared aloof made the chase more exciting. When I tired during the seven months of the chase I found plenty of distractions. And here I was in her town. It was my town for seven years and ours for five. It was a town that I knew well, one that was as familiar to me now as it was then. The new one way systems, shopping centres and parking restrictions tried to put me off the scent but the memories were too strong.

I had come to see her and I was close. I wasn't sure what I should say when I met her. The fact that she lived with her sister suggested that she was still single. I took comfort in that although eighteen years is a long time. A lot could have happened in that time. At least we would have something to talk about.

A little girl came and sat on the bench. She must have been four or five years old. She wore a tea shirt with a dinosaur and a little pleated skirt.

'Hello, sweetheart,' I smiled, 'and what's your name?'

'Debbie.'

'Well, I am pleased to meet you Debbie.'

Just then I heard a shout from the other side of the playground. 'Debbie, come here now!'

Her mother walked across to us. She grabbed her by the hand and pulled her away.

'It's alright,' I said, 'she wasn't bothering me'.

'Yeah, I am sure she wasn't.' She snarled. 'I've told you not to talk to strangers!'

I felt uncomfortable. I got up and walked out of the playground. I had made a mistake. I had made an embarrassing mistake.

I was in unfamiliar territory and had ignored the fact that there were a lot of sick people around that young mothers had to protect their offspring from. Every week there was some incident involving a child and here I was making an acquaintance without being introduced.

More than that, I was in a strange town, trying to look up a friend after eighteen years and, comfortable with the fact that she, having lived without needing me for at least seventeen of those years, should meet me because I had nothing to do. I was angry at my insensitivity. I should not be here. I speeded up my pace away from the block. I needed to get to the main road where I had parked the car. My heart sank. I wished I had Joan to go back to.

IV

'Hello Sarah, how are you. It has been a long time hasn't it.'

Sarah didn't say a word. She had aged. Her hair was not as tidy as it used to be and she had put on a little weight.

'You haven't changed. In fact you look just the same as the last day I saw you,' I said.

Sarah turned and walked away. She didn't say a word. It seems that the dream was real but she was not. I left. We never became friends.

*　　　*　　　*

Intrusions

I

Privacy is something that we all value. At some time or other in our lives it is the invasion of that privacy that causes upheaval and it is the relationships with the outside world that by their very nature intrude in that arena. Although it is said to mean different things to different people I have found that not to be the case. There is as far as I can see something that is common to all the people I have come across and in particular the response to any possible loss is regarded as a great tragedy of, in some cases, classical Greek proportions. Thus, in the world in which I find that people with whom I interact walk through this life balancing the demands of their secret lives with the perception of themselves that they are so desperate to maintain. Some get away with it and achieve the epithet 'Beloved Husband and Father, forever missed. RIP' while others live too long for secrets to remain hidden.

Such was an encounter with a young man with whom I fell in love. You may understand that love to be platonic to make it easier for you to accept. He was twenty-six years old, slight of build with an Englishness that comes of reading too much Jane Austen. Double cuffed shirts that I always assumed to have been starched, slightly tired collars and a lazy tie knot, all that gave the impression of good breeding. My twenty years too many didn't seem to matter because we were comfortable together. I have always held that age was always the other persons' problem because I was never consciously aware of it. As long as the other person didn't have a problem with it why should I?

We met at those obvious of all places, work. He had just joined us in the finance department and, being on the same floor as our marketing department, he was taken around by his director to be introduced to us.

I remember the very first time that I saw him I felt he looked the part, pin-striped shirt, a suit that was obviously not off the peg and hair brushed back in a casual manner that no stylist could have improved on and, most importantly, a level of confidence that was most attractive. His physical features are hard to describe, not because I have forgotten them, how could I ever! but because the only words that I can call on for help are words that have so often been used that they provide nothing more than a Hollywood stereotype which would give the reader the wrong image.

I spoke to him the first time at the coffee machine. I noticed he took his coffee sweet. That suited him. I don't know why but he was the first to speak to me. Perhaps he had caught me staring.

'Hi, you must be Dave in marketing.'

Surprised as I was that he spoke to me I was even more so because he remembered my name and the department I worked in.

'So how are you finding it? It must be difficult. After all, with over three hundred on this floor it will take some time to get to know everyone.'

I realized as soon as I said it that it was a stupid thing to say. Why on earth would anyone try to get to know everyone of those three hundred people that inhabited a space which at its broadest could take three minutes to walk across? Christmas parties were the best reminder of how few colleagues we end up getting to know.

We talked while the coffee machine discreetly buzzed through its processes. Charles sipped his coffee while I waited for mine to appear. We went through our introductions gently throwing out information that the other could test to see whether there was anything in common and if so whether it would be worth investing in the relationship. It was called networking and the coffee machine was as good a place as any to practice it.

The days passed gently by as we got to know each other. The finance team planned to go out for a drink and Charles rang to ask whether I would like to come along. I didn't know very many people in finance but agreed on the basis that Charles was going to be there. It was fun. Douglas, the finance director was there and was pleased to see me there as an example of departments mixing. He asked me with affected interest about what I was up to and listened when I told him. I liked talking about my work, what the competition was up to and what we were doing in retaliation. He talked to me as if I were a lot younger than I was and even said how he enjoyed the enthusiasm of youth. That remark threw me for a second because he was only seven or eight years older than me but then I enjoyed the moment. I always liked it when people thought I was younger than I was. I think it has something to do with the satisfaction of marriage and children that encourages a middle age spread, unkempt hair and the indulgence of flirting and being patronizing at the same time.

I had married young and am pleased to say it had been a disaster from the start. I had acted the part of the husband in love and particularly enjoyed helping in the kitchen, making Alison breakfast in bed and meeting her friends. The only part I dreaded was going to bed when I knew another obligation was required. Alison was not that demanding and I somehow was able to bear it with undisclosed anxiety. She did sometimes question why I wasn't the animal that men were supposed to be but somehow I got away with that too. I think the only thing that she never forgave me was the calmness with which I let her go. The divorce was easy. There were no children and I was not prepared to fight for anything we had together. The only thing I insisted on was not paying any alimony and as she had already converted a lover into a prospective husband she soon gave up trying. I was thirty-three and she a year younger than me. I enjoyed my life of ease, at peace with myself and a group of friends that were delightful company when I needed them. I had treated myself to an old Mercedes sports car which I enjoyed looking after and driving around. Bright red both in colour and temperament she was a delight. Charles and I spent a lovely summer driving around the country which apart from a couple of unpleasant incidents born of prejudice still remains a perfect memory.

We became lovers by accident. He was my first and the first time that I ever felt the pleasure of going to bed.

Charles had come over to my flat after a trip to the theatre. We both loved Oscar Wilde and the performance of The Importance of Being Ernest' was brilliant. I lived just off the Fulham Rd and being a Friday night there was no rush to get home. I asked whether he would like to come over and we could have a salad that I could make. Charles agreed provided I would let him drive the car. I laughed at the thought of indulging him with something as simple as his request. The evening was still fun and there seemed no reason to end it just because the planned part of the evening was over. On the way back we picked up a bottle of claret. Charles loved claret.

Charles got the drinks and I made the salad. We talked of the show and of the brilliance of Oscar Wilde. We talked of his conversion born of a search for an excitement that success, a perfect marriage and the adoration of all could not provide. It was light hearted at first, then intellectual and finally sad. We were both a little drunk too but that didn't stop me from being a little surprised when he kissed me. Perhaps I was too drunk to resist, perhaps merely curious to see how far it would go but all the same I wonder even now why I was not repulsed by it. For forty-six years I had lived according to a prejudice that even the changing society that I lived in couldn't eradicate and yet when it came to it I did not resist. I haven't had the opportunity to find out whether that is the case with others and would love to find out some day. It was that day we became lovers.

No-one suspected. Somehow unless one comes out bluntly admitting it everyone assumes there to be nothing in it. We were good friends in the office and shared interests and therefore it was natural that we should meet after work. We still went for drinks with the guys and passed comment on rumours about the exploits of colleagues. It wasn't hard to carry on as if nothing had changed, not for a while at least.

It was a remark that Douglas passed that I suppose put us on notice.

'Where are you two off to? You're not gay are you?'

'Why, Douglas, making you jealous?'

We laughed.

That night, lying in bed, I asked Charles what he made of the joke, whether they suspected. Charles was tired. He looked so peaceful in my arms. He said he didn't care.

It was true Charles didn't really care. He was young; it wasn't his first time and thought I was making a big thing out of nothing. I knew I wasn't and it was a big thing. There is one thing living in this world according to the norms and quite another living as one's heart moved one. The same prejudice that accompanied relationships formed between two people of different ethnic origins or religions existed in the case of a mix of genders. We lived in a free society that allowed people to live as they were capable of living but not without paying the extra price demanded of acceptance by 'normal' people. Gide, in the 'Immoralist', was pandering to that particular demand in switching the genders of the lovers to what was considered acceptable. If he hadn't done that he would not have been able to tell the story at the time he had written it nor would it have made such a passionate read now that everyone knows where his preferences lay.

I suppose that was when things started proving more difficult. I made a conscious effort to avoid the relaxed manner in which I would meet up with Charles for lunch. We did that for a month or so. I could see the strain that Charles was under. He didn't say anything to warn me so it came as a surprise when he told me that he had received an offer for a job at another company. He said he needed a change and although the job was not much better than the one he had he had accepted. Douglas asked me to see him after Charles had handed in his resignation.

'Listen, I know it is none of my business and I do not

want to pry but everyone knows you to be a good friend to Charles. Do you know why he wants to move?'

I think I came across as unhelpful but there wasn't anything I could say to him. After all I didn't know why Charles was leaving. In fact I was hurt that he had not confided in me.

The leaving party was a riot. We all got very drunk and Douglas was generous with the drinks. He paid for most of them. Obviously on expenses but still he didn't have to. I was beginning to feel sick and decided to leave while I would still be able to find my own way home. I thought Charles would come over that night but he didn't.

I had the most awful hangover the next day and rang in to say that I wasn't well. Our secretary said she had heard that half the finance department had rung in with the same excuse.

I rang Charles in the afternoon but there was no reply. He was still sleeping it off. It wasn't until about nine that evening when he rang me.

'Hi, I have just got up. How are you?'

'I couldn't go into work today.'

'Wimp! And you left early. Lack staying power.' He tried to laugh but didn't make it.

Neither of us had the energy to meet up so we agreed to meet for dinner the next day. Charles had a few days off before starting his new job. I felt a lot better the next day and so did Charles, brave enough at least to order a bottle of wine. It was an evening that I will never forget. Never in my life had anyone made me such a sacrifice or demonstration of love. Charles started the conversation. He was a little nervous. I, as always, feared the worst. It was too good to last.

'Now I can tell you why I changed jobs.' He played with his soup.

'Jeff, I'm taking a chance on this. I'm in love with you.'

I remember how the tears ran down my cheeks. I got up and kissed him. It turned a few heads in the restaurant I am sure but quite honestly at the time I didn't care.

He had given up his job because he had felt that sooner or later it would become difficult for us to go on with our relationship. Charles came home that night and moved in by the end of the week.

II

It didn't take long for those in the office to find out. It was strange that they didn't put two and two together. I suppose the idea that someone would leave because they wanted the freedom to love without the risk of being caught out was too romantic for this day and age. They joked about it with me on a one to one basis, called me a sly devil, and generally showed a concerned acceptance which 'other people' sometimes found difficult. I hesitated about confiding in any of them for a while because I wasn't sure how they really felt about it. My boss was well trained in people management and took time out after a meeting to let me know that as far as he was concerned ones sexual preference didn't matter to him so long as it didn't affect their work, knew that I was a professional and I would ensure that to be the case. It was so clichéd I almost made the mistake of laughing at the seriousness with which he was making his point but thankfully self restraint prevailed and I managed to thank him for being so understanding.

The next few weeks were blissful. I longed to go home and Charles was always there looking as wonderful as he did the very first time I saw him. The memory of it is I am sure embellished as wonderful memories are but that makes it all the more precious. I think one only embellishes memories that are wonderful and that becomes in my view an affirmation which in its own way adds rather than takes away anything from the pleasure.

We settled down into a very pleasant existence which within the confines of our flat brought us out of ourselves. It was like living a dream.

Charles refused to come out to drinks with people from

work and although I chided him for it, I didn't insist. I still wasn't sure what people really felt about our relationship and didn't want the embarrassment of having to deal with any remarks that a few beers might, as harmless as they may have been intended to be, would hurt us. Reality was, I was sure, unkind and I thought it might break the spell so that we would see each ourselves as we really were, a middle aged faggot with a young man that was disgusting despite the Victorian values having been pronounced dead for at least fifty years.

We went out to restaurants as would two colleagues from work and refrained from any behaviour that might give us away. Friends, and it did come as a surprise that Charles had so many, were whittled down to a bare minimum and even then none that we could be ourselves with. I suppose that is when I noticed the age difference between us. Young people have an energy which from the outside I also found attractive as was the irreverence with which they berated middle class values. When I was introduced to them, the shallowness of their arguments and the arrogance with which they universally agreed a position irritated me. At first I found it endearing in a patronizing sort of way but then it grew tiresome and I would start searching for a way in which I could suggest to Charles that we should leave without ending up making a scene. Charles was good about it to begin with but then I began to sense a disappointment which hurt. I repaid that with gratitude and loved him the more for it although I could never be sure that he thought it a fair exchange.

It was different with my friends. Whereas Charles was happy me meeting his friends I was uneasy when he met mine. I could sense the disapproval and soon ended trying any sort of integration. I suppose we both sacrificed our friends for the relationship that we so much needed and over just a few weeks managed to become prisoners in our own home. We laughed about being under house arrest. It was a sad joke because of the truth in it. I suppose we both knew that such a relationship might in the ordinary scheme of things be unsustainable but ours was a special love that had to endure. I liked being with Charles and he with me. We vowed to be together forever and were determined to make our dream come true.

This is not a love story that starts with a special attraction and ends with a relationship becoming stale through boredom. This is a story about two people who find it hard to come to terms with the reality of social acceptance. I was not gay when this began. I had no intention of ever becoming attracted to a man and yet when it did happen all those years of prejudice did nothing to prevent it. I loved as would anyone else. The fact that the object of my attraction was of the same sex as myself was something that I found natural. The shock of our relationship was not how we showed our love for each other in the private confines of our home but how we were seen from the outside. Years of hearing jokes about gay men, serious conversations that turned to pity or anger that ended in either disgust or ridicule had taught me to hear them again about us. I looked for the signs in faces of friends, the actions of strangers and finally in the questioning of my own feelings when work forced us to be apart for any length of time.

Time passed and lethargy crept in. It was a tiring relationship when every day we would have to devise some means of behaving as normal people. Neighbours at first thought I had taken in a flat mate. The same neighbours that had confined our acquaintance to a polite 'hello' or 'good morning' began to find it too difficult to retain the affected pleasantries that city life so proudly cultivates. At first I thought it was my imagination and then Charles began to notice it too. The old, to whom I have always shown the deference my mother taught me, were the most obvious. Heterosexual friends who worried about me being alone for so long and who tried to set me up with a plethora of eligible women could not find it in themselves to rejoice at my finding the happiness they had for so long wished for me.

We were happy together in our Garden of Eden. Life was honest in our home but then our home was not the world. Real life intruded and three weeks before our first anniversary Charles left me for someone else. He said it was not my fault and I thank him for saying so.

* * *

The Dream

The dream was one of those that I couldn't explain. I had a decent relationship in which I had lasted four years without much to complain of. He was kind, considerate and whenever I totted up all that he gave me I couldn't imagine anyone else giving me nearly as much. The material pleasures of an economically dependent marriage were of course not all that I had dreamed of but were more than most of the friends I had been to school with could boast. My failure to have children was something that was hard to come to grips with but the fact that I was the one to blame added to my contentment. He never mentioned it as something that I should feel guilty about although in my heart I knew that an unfortunate abortion was probably the cause. I never told him about it. It wasn't necessary as there are many things that one does in the past which have no relevance to the present. I am not enough of a romantic to believe that a good marriage is based on a clean start following a confession.

The dream worried me though. It was the first of its kind since we had been together and if he had not woken me up at the time he did I am sure that I would not have remembered it.

I was at a party. The drinks were plentiful and free, the sort that allows consumption without the need for pretence in respect of quality or taste, just the sort that is needed when the sole purpose is to get over inhibitions as quickly as possible. There were a number of Americans at the party and a few Japanese. Both similar in terms of being loud enough to make sure that the rest of us could enjoy ourselves in the knowledge that whatever we did we would still be seen to be the relatively quieter bunch. I liked being around Americans at social gatherings. It is not nice to generalize but then how else do we ever form opinions that can be expounded in a social setting and not end up in an argument or a fight. There are of course rules such as never generalize about anyone within earshot or if you do make sure that you do not make it personal by making it political, gender related, religious or ethnic.

The scene switched to a room with two builders. I was in the room with them. They were fixing two ceiling lights, one in the wrong place. I told them they were making a mistake. They told me that they had been given clear instructions by my husband which they were following correctly. I told them to listen to me but they wouldn't, those horrible smelly people. I tried to leave the room but couldn't find a door. They laughed at me.

The scene switched to a field. I was chasing someone. I don't know who it was. He was young. It was a hot day. He tripped and fell and I fell on top of him. The scene changed. We were making love. I was on top. I was trying to make it happen for him but couldn't. The more I tried the more I saw the anguish in his eyes intensify. He had a rock in his hand. I was scared he was going to hit me with it. It was green, emerald green. I still didn't recognise his face. I don't know why I am telling you about this or why it should bother me but it does.

I do not believe in the interpretation of dreams. I know I had seen a film with my husband just before we went to bed. We didn't make love for menstrual reasons. The film had a party scene and a sex scene. I was very tired as I always am during these times. I know that dreams often end up being a 'cut and paste' of things that had happened during the day. It was the first time I remembered such a dream after waking up.

The dream worried me. I didn't want it to worry me. My husband gave me a let out yesterday. He told me he had a strange dream. I told him I had a scary dream the same night. He told me to tell him about the dream but I asked him to go first.

He dreamt that he had woken in the middle of the night from a scary dream. The room was dark. Even though the curtains were drawn he could tell it was still night. A winters' night that blacked out city lights. He could hear that

I was watching television in the sitting room downstairs. It was a realty show that I loved watching and always irritated the hell out of him. He wanted to call out to me but when he tried he couldn't hear his voice. He couldn't move or speak. He could hear me laughing out loud. He saw strange forms on the ceiling smiling down at him. When he woke up he found me snoring next to him. His heart was beating at a thousand beats a minute. He cuddled up to me. I stopped snoring and said something in my sleep which he couldn't make out. He didn't remember falling asleep but when he woke up he remembered the dream. He didn't think anything of it but today at work he remembered the dream. He remembered it again on his way home and again just before the moment that he wanted to tell me about it.

I told him I thought it was a strange dream but it didn't seem to mean anything. He agreed with me and asked me to tell him about my dream. I did.

He asked me whether I knew who it had been, how old he was, where he was while all this was happening. I told him.

My husband is always supportive. He agreed it was a strange dream. He told me that no one has ever found out why we dream or what dreams signify. I reminded him of Joseph and the Bible. We both laughed, neither of us are believers.

He asked me a strange question today. He asked me whether he thought we had good sex together. I said I thought it was fine. I asked him why he had asked the question. He said that he sometimes felt that he was not able to satisfy me. I told him that he was being silly and asked him to change the subject.

After dinner he asked me whether I loved him. He often asks me that question. In fact we both ask each other the question. It is rhetorical actually but we both wait for an answer. The answers are automatic and predictable. I think we have asked each other the question so often we no longer hear the answer.

Today was one of those days when nothing very much happened. We had a day at work, came home, tried to watch television but there wasn't much on. We weren't in the mood for a film and decided to have an early night. We tried to make love although I wasn't quite done with my condition. I told him I wasn't quite done but he didn't listen. I was too tired to put a fight so let him get on with it. He didn't make it. I knew he would be upset but there was nothing I could do.

It was too early to go to sleep. We weren't tired enough. He decided to get up. I didn't make a sound. He sighed as he left the room. I heard him go downstairs and switch on the television. He was channel hopping. I could hear it.

I was still awake when he came back to bed half an hour later.

'Are you asleep?'

'No.'

'What a strange day'

'Yes.'

There was a silence while we both searched for something to say.

'Never mind sweetheart,' I said, 'tomorrow will be another day.'

I kissed him on the shoulder as he turned away from me. I assumed the spoon position and hoped that tomorrow everything would be alright.

*   *   *

The End of Summer

I

It was a long time coming. Both of them had been expecting it but when the end came, it came suddenly. They had been living a life that had the sustainability of a dream. This story is not about death or divorce, or some other natural disaster that relationships are prone to. It is a story of the illness that sustains the life of normality. An illness that sets in when couples are encouraged by routine to take a chance on making a change for which there is no reason other than possibly the need to get rid of a boredom that creeps in and irritates like 'pins and needles'. It occurs at a time when a future free of fear seems almost attainable.

They had been together for just over seven years. The significant events of seven years could now be recounted to new acquaintances without feeling. The first meeting, the falling in love, the quarrel with the family, the moving in, the first fight and so on. It was nothing new and both would recount the history of the relationship as if it were some badly written novella by an up and coming soon to be forgotten writer of great promise. This was a love of great promise, and like many similar stories of loves past, this had too fallen prey to the comfort of familiarity.

II

The dog had been a birthday present. Judy couldn't remember whether she had asked for one or whether it was John that wanted one but it was Judy that got the present. The event exuded excitement. The sitcom sketch of becoming parents of an animal that was bred for the purpose, sold and paid for in the cause of recreation. Now, John had become a daddy and Judy a mummy of a golden retriever puppy two months old. It was like the real thing! They took six weeks to decide on the name for the dog. This time neither could remember who came up with the name except that P G Woodhouse was somehow responsible. Judy assumed that John would keep Bertie. He was more fond of the dog and anyway she wanted a clean break. No ties with the past.

'You can keep Bertie,' said Judy with an abruptness born of the fear that John might be thinking the same.

'I don't want him.'

'What will you do with him?'

'Ring the RSPCA.'

Judy didn't bite. She knew he was trying to get at her. John loved Bertie. He always took him out in the mornings. He never complained. He would leave Judy taking her 'precious fifteen' minutes as she called it to rouse herself to greet the day. 'Come on Bertie, leave lazy bones in bed,' and John would jump into his tracksuit and off they would go. Judy was always grateful for that half an hour without them in the morning. She knew that there was something she had to be grateful to Bertie for and yes that was it, allowing her half an hour to come to terms with the reality that was on offer.

III

The first sign things were not going well came with a present Judy had bought for herself. John hadn't thought through why he was so annoyed. It had crossed his mind that he should think about it before giving an instinctive response but then the discussion had developed into an argument and then into a 'full scale' row almost as if it had a life of its own. He was powerless to control it. Every time he opened his mouth things got worse and suddenly John found himself standing in front of the car with the car keys in his hand wondering how he had got there. He recalled slamming the door, calling her a stupid bitch but couldn't remember why. What was worse he didn't want to go anywhere. It was past ten in the evening and all he really wanted to do was to watch some TV and then go to bed. Nothing was going to happen tonight.

But there he was outside his house, in front of his car, Judy in the house crying, Bertie still barking away in his futile attempt to understand what was going on and John, still with nowhere to go.

Angry at having been put in that position John decided that he was not going to accept it. Why did he have to leave the house? It was more his than hers. He had paid more of the deposit for the house when they had bought it five years ago. He wouldn't lose face if he just turned and walked back. He would ignore her, wouldn't even look at her, walk straight past her without acknowledging that she was there. Go up to bed and go to sleep. He looked at his watch. It was still only just past ten. A little early but John remembered how that morning he had thought that he could really do with a good nights sleep. Well here was his chance. It would be an earlier night than he expected but still that is what he wanted.

He turned towards the house. The front garden looked nice in the yellow and white of the street lighting. He had done a good job at the weekend, John and Bertie that is. Bertie was a good listener and it was nice having some-one around when he was working in the garden. Judy had wanted a lie in. The evening had been fun. Roger and Claire were always a laugh but they hadn't got home until after two in the morning. It was stupid of John to have tried. He should have expected that Judy wouldn't be interested. He hated Judy making excuses. He always felt like a schoolboy caught trying to catch a glimpse of a girl's bra or knickers and promised that he would never get caught again. He huffed that every time he was in the mood, she wasn't! He told himself that it wasn't sex that he was interested in. It was love and when she didn't want to do it was because she didn't love him.

He opened the front door to the noise of the television loud enough to drown what had just happened. It irritated John. Judy didn't care. As far as she was concerned, he thought, she was trying to tell him she didn't care.

He went stomping up the stairs to let her know he was going upstairs. He didn't notice any reaction.

He changed his clothes and got into bed. Bertie had gone into the sitting room to Judy. Fickle as he was looking for attention wherever he could get it. Lying in bed he listened to the television downstairs. He could hear it was a 'sitcom' but couldn't make out which one. He heard the canned laughter but couldn't hear Judy's laughter. John tried to concentrate on sleeping but the television distracted him. He switched on the bedside lamp. It was a nice IKEA lamp with a blue ceramic base. Judy had chosen it. John felt sad as he remembered the love he felt for Judy and wondered what he should have done differently to make her love him as much as he loved her. He hated these domestic scenes. He didn't like arguing with her. He remembered what it was like before he met her. The lonely nights that taunted him. He loved her so desperately and yet was able in a moment to change everything. He was angry but still loved her. He wanted things to be normal. He didn't want to continue like this.

He got out of bed and went downstairs. The sitcom was still on. It was just past eleven and yet he felt that an age had already passed. He walked into the sitting room. Judy was sitting on the sofa staring at the television.

'You know Judy, things can't go on like this.'

Judy ignored him.

I don't know what you want. Why don't you tell me? Why do we have to fight like this?

Judy continued to ignore him. John was caught again. He didn't know what to do. He wanted her attention but didn't know how to get it.

He walked over to the television and switched it off. Judy continued to look at the blank screen of the television.

'Do you want to end it?'

Judy smiled. It wasn't an affectionate smile but a smile that hinted at boredom. It was smile that did it. A new row began. This time John backed down for fear that the neighbours would call the police. He left the room and went upstairs. The television was on by the time he got into bed again. He felt sorry for himself. He was power-less. His physical and psychological control over Judy once again proved to be less than he imagined. He had lost again.

John was late home for the next few days. He found work that needed to be done, joined colleagues for a drink or found a pub to have a drink.

Then Judy wore make-up, cooked him dinner and with the calculated moves that come with good planning and rehearsal ensured that they made love and everything was back to normal. The migraine had passed and the memory of the pain that they had gone through disintegrated until the next row that would take place a few weeks later.

Again the reason for the row, as with all the rows they had was incidental. A marriage guidance counsellor would have helped but they were not married. They had no ex-cuses to make a big thing of it. They were living together and could end it whenever they wanted to. That was the reason John had never proposed to Judy and he regret-ted it.

The row was not the first but it was different. The effect of it lasted. It was like the smell of musty clothes that lin-gered all day, the smell of decomposing flesh or the smell of death.

IV

The end came suddenly. They both knew it had hap-pened but it still came as a surprise.

John was to go away to a conference. Judy had agreed that she would accompany him. He was sure of that. It was when John had reminded Judy about the conference that the end came. Judy didn't want to go. He had booked the hotel, told his colleagues and his boss that she was coming. Now that John had got everything organized Judy didn't want to go.

Judy knew that she had said yes and in the argument

that followed admitted that she had now changed her mind. She was not being vindictive. She just didn't want to go. She had accompanied him once before two years ago and hated it. She sat around in the hotel while he attended his meetings and then attended the dinners where the conversation was not only superficial but repetitive. She regretted agreeing to go with John in the first place and if he had wanted to listen would have explained why she had changed her mind. It was when he started pleading with her that she had became stubborn. She knew that she was being unnecessarily brutal with him but couldn't stop. It was always the same. She repeatedly said no and nothing he could do could change her mind. She made no excuses. She just did not want to go and that was it.

John went to the conference alone. He didn't like it. It seemed as if everyone was with a spouse. He drank too much which didn't help. He thought of Judy but didn't ring her on principle.

When he got back she wore make-up. Helped him unpack and they made love. It was back to normal again but the smell remained.

V

The reasons for the arguments were never known. No effort was made to understand them. They weren't even sure that if they had tried it would have ever been possible. Life became better. John enjoyed a drink with his colleagues. Judy went on ladies nights out. They made love when the appetite arose. They argued but Judy never failed to put on the make-up when required. The clean break never came.

*   *   *

The Visit

I was late for my psychiatrist. I worried because he didn't like to be kept waiting and I wondered whether it would be worth just not turning up with some excuse. I was good at making excuses. With over forty two years on this planet and having been late all my life I learned from experience. That was not the issue today. I knew that sooner or later I would come clean with him and then face the embarrassment of having lied to someone I was told I was not allowed to lie to.

When I got to his office exaggerating regret at being late his secretary did as she was told and kept me waiting for another ten minutes. It was to teach me a lesson and I understood that. It wasn't the first time I had been dealt that kind of punishment.

'Sorry to keep you waiting John'.

'That is alright,' I said. 'I am sorry I was late. The buses, the tube, my leg hurt, I hurt my back, my watch was slow or any other excuse that you would like today.'

He was still looking at a letter and although had acknowledged my presence in words had still to look up at me to confirm that he knew I was there. He held that position long enough for me to notice that his pupils were not moving across the letter in front of him. The punishment was obviously continuing but I knew at the end of the day he had no way to win. I was here for my session which I had not wanted to attend anyway and if he wanted to get paid he would have to do something. His patience lasted for thirty seconds and then with an affected smile he looked up and asked me to take a seat.

It was my wife that forced me to go and see the doctor. I realised only after the event that she had already spoken to the doctor about my condition. When he scared me into believing that I was going through some ghastly mental crisis I agreed with the help of my wife to see the psychiatrist.

I had been registered for six sessions. The two that I had already attended were a waste of time. The first one John, he asked to me call him John rather than Doctor Inwich, had spent all the time talking about what he was going to do and the second had been spent with me answering predictable open questions about my current state of being, my relationship with my wife (sexual and otherwise), my work which just about took the hour that the session was planned for.

'Well Mike, how are you feeling?'

I generally hate stupid banal questions. How does one ever feel? I am forty-two years old, married with a wife that loves me, have two beautiful children and a job that I am not in the process of losing. 'How do I feel?' Well, if I was fine why would my wife think I am going crazy? Why would she arrange for me to see a doctor who in turn would shun his responsibility and send me to a psychiatrist.

'Fine, thanks. How are you?'

I am not really going mad. I somehow miss the excitement in everything. Losing interest. My wife is good to me. She offers me sex when I want it, my children remind me that I am their father and need me when they have nothing to do. My job is fine. I get paid a lot for fulfilling a routine.

'What have you been up to?'

I can't remember whether John answered my question. I think he must have and I assume that to be the case.

'Nothing much.'

John is a typical psychiatrist. His hair a mess and his clothes look as if they could have done with a dry-clean years ago. I wonder what his life is like. What pleasure does he get from living. He told me he had a wife and children but reminded me that I was there to talk about me.

I wanted to oblige but wasn't sure what to talk about. I was sinking into the quagmire of a world where everything happens around me. I had nothing to contribute except to keep the status quo. Keep going even though I knew that it was all a game which I didn't enjoy playing.

II

I can't remember who said it but the law is an ass! I don't know why I said that but it is true.

'Well you must have been up to something, why don't you tell me what's been happening at work?'

Now there is a question for you, encouraging me to make up something.

'Nothing much. The same old client issues. Some clients happy others not. Some pay on time others repeat excuses that millions before them have made. My boss is happy. My colleagues don't bother me much. I get to work on time and leave an hour late. The coffee still tastes awful. I get paid on time. I am not in line for a promotion for at least three years so I can breathe easy. I don't have to go 'brown nosing' or make a fool of myself like those poor cretins around me.'

I didn't want to make anything up. After all he is a poor man just trying to do his job. The fact that he doesn't care isn't his problem. He doesn't get to choose his patients, does he?

'Do you think you deserve promotion earlier than the three years you think you will have to wait?'

It was another stupid question. I knew if he carried on like this he was going to lose any sympathy that I might have for him.

'Not really,' I said trying to deflect any compulsion to make up something.

'Happy at home?'

You know I never wanted to come and see a psychiatrist. If it wasn't for Mary raising the matter with our GP and the GP threatening to force me to seek help. If I didn't do so voluntarily I wouldn't have been there. I was surprised that he could force me and his explanation of his power on this matter was frightening. I didn't get angry with Mary because the harm had been done. I was also a little scared because it is not pleasant to have a wife who betrays you. You haven't really got a hope. It is not as easy to get rid of a wife as it may seem. She can steal from you, have as many affairs as she can accommodate and still get at least half of what you have saved, invested and all of what you have created except of course visiting rights which really are an insult.

'Yes, thank you. I have a great supportive wife, two lovely children and a dog,' I lied.

'I thought the dog died a few months ago?'

'I mean I had a dog' I said, trying to recover from the slip up.

'How did the dog die?'

He knew the dog had died and also without doubt knew how he had died. That question was the start. He was beginning to annoy me.

Mary had taken the children swimming and I was left at home all alone. I had decided to mow the front lawn and the dog had come out to help. Idiot. I never liked the scruffy old mongrel and tolerated him only because the children doted on him. I sometimes suspected that Mary liked the dog more than she liked me. She was probably into bestiality or something because he certainly got more attention than I did.

I used to call him 'Dog' half in a weak attempt at showing my feelings for him and partly to tease Mary and the children.

'Dad, his name is Trevor!'

'Whose darling?' I would ask hiding behind a newspaper.

'Our dogs'!'

Then they would run off to their mother complaining bitterly that I was being unkind to the dog. Mary was an idiot because she would fall for it and start shouting at me to stop tormenting the children. What began as a little tease would end up being a full blown row with the children crying, the dog wining and doors slamming. It was in those situations that I would find myself outside my own house with not an idea of what I was supposed to do next. It is difficult to go anywhere when you are annoyed, want to make a point and haven't got a clue how to go about it especially when you know you will have to come back to face the music.

The dog had been playing with the water and irritating the hell out of me. I turned up the radio in the manner of teenagers that believe the whole world is waiting to hear what they have discovered. It helped drown out some of the noise that the dog was making.

The next thing I heard was the screaming of the children and Mary shouting at me. I turned to find that the beast had been run over by a car and there was a general commotion in the street. I suffered accusations of neglect, cruelty to animals, irresponsibility and the promise that I would be made to pay for it which I did over the next few weeks. The children refused to speak to me. The food I ate was meant for the dog and the conjugal bliss was more what would be expected by a eunuch in a brothel!

'Are you alright Mike?'

'Yes I am fine. Thanks. And you?'

'I am fine too John. Don't you want to talk about the dog?'

'Oh sorry, he got run over.'

'Well, that was a good session, wasn't it? I think we made progress. See you again on Thursday. You take it easy now, won't you?'

III

I left his office not really sure what I was supposed to do.

Mary had been kinder to me ever since I had started these sessions. I got the occasional kiss and a cuddle in front of the children but that was it. Mary still made sure we went to bed at different times and any advances made in bed were repulsed with feminine ease of either snoring or bludgeoning hints of tiredness. Although annoying at first I had got into the habit of drooling about someone in the office or starting an erotic dream with elements of a pornographic film I had seen many years ago.

It was three o'clock in the afternoon. I could go back to work but as they did not expect me back I had the opportunity to skive off. If I had a wife at home I could always go home and perhaps sneak one in before the children came home. The thought amused me, I remember.

I stood there in the street watching the crowds rushing off in all direction as if with some purpose. I too wanted a purpose. I wanted to go somewhere. I wanted to have somewhere to get to. I wanted to have too much to do so that I could be like everyone else and complain about not having enough time. I wanted a mortgage that kept me desperately tied to my job or a wife and children that demanded more than I could give them. I wanted to contribute to something, anything.

A pretty girl across the road caught my attention. I watched her figure dance the gestures of walking along the road with provocation; breasts and legs in perfect harmony. Her age didn't matter. I saw her walk into a travel shop. I don't know why but I found myself crossing the road and following her into the shop.

All the assistants were busy and she was sitting in what was a waiting area. I sat down too discreetly leaving an empty chair between us. I smiled as I sat down.

'Have you been waiting long,' I asked.

'No, not very long.'

I couldn't think of anything else I could get away with asking without raising her alarm bells so I sat there in silence watching the holiday needs of the debris of human society being met by packaged tours that wouldn't tax their mental agility. Both young and old alike, family holidays and singles, were all catered for to ensure expectations were met; domestic needs satisfied by taking the stress out of a family holiday, pensioners given the impression that they had more to wait for than physical disability and death, singles given an artificial environment which increased their chances of getting laid, and yuppies with carefully packaged adventure holidays with life and limb insurance that they could impress colleagues and friends with.

A lady came up to me to ask whether she could help. I said I didn't know and leaving her with a puzzled look and with as much dignity as I could I left the shop.

IV

They found me in Brighton. In a little bedsit usually reserved for foreigners on a cheap visit to a famous seaside resort. I had been betrayed by my landlord but only after he had taken all the money I had. I had apparently been there two weeks and the thousand pounds I had been allowed to take out of our joint account from the building society had already been spent. I didn't realise that fish and chip, which was my staple diet for the whole two weeks, could cost so much.

The hospital I was at was an old Victorian hospital for the mentally insane. It was a nice hospital and the nurses provided me with enough dirty thoughts to keep me distracted when I was on my own. I had nothing to do except take the pills they gave me, watch television, and do what I was told at other times.

Mary came to see me twice a week. She was happy because the health insurance I had covered us at full salary for the first six months and at half salary for the next six. After that the redundancy package and social security would ensure an easy life.

The children didn't come because at their tender age it would be too disturbing for them. I understood. Besides they had a new dog to look after.

*   *   *

Ganesh

He sat there looking at Anil. The green Ganesh soap dish that Anil had disliked from the first time he had seen it. Ganesh, a Hindu god that was the subject of great reverence for his mother had been reduced to being an ornament on a soap dish! He didn't like Ganesh watching him wash away the illicit love making that the tradition he had been brought up in would never accept. The soap dish matched the green shower curtains with small white flowers that Anil had bought with Romala on one of those domestic occasions when they had almost felt married.

For Anil it was a convenient arrangement. Apart from the soap dish there was not much retribution. Romala was the perfect mate. Always available when he had the opportunity and never complained. Every man's dream really, all the bliss of marriage without the commitment. It was like having other people's children over that were potty trained and could be given back when one tired of the experience.

The occasional guilt, if there was any, was soon forgotten when he flirted with other girls and could say, with hand on heart, that he was single.

He came out of the bathroom wearing a towel and drying his hair. He had consciously picked that up that from the movies they watched together. They always used two bath towels in the movies. It took him a while to teach Romala to leave two bath towels for him and now they were always there.

Romala was still asleep, sprawled on the bed as if posing for a painting that would in the name of art provide the voyeurs of the world a patronizing excuse to ogle. The bed sheets tightly wrapped around her legs and shoulders allowed Anil to see her as a package beautifully wrapped. Her hair, shoulder length, fell about her in the careless manner that only a sensitive director could arrange. Loose curls, pitch black, that set off her golden skin born of the marriage that came from the drive of encouraged immigration of the fifties. Anil needed to go. He was late.

As he left the flat he felt pleased with himself. It was a good evening; the night delivered the opportunity he expected and he was off to work.

II

'You're bright and early.'

'Oh, hi Monika. Yes I couldn't sleep,' Anil lied through a smile.

Monika was pretty in a familiar sort of way. She was confident about her body and displayed just enough to not be too much. She liked the idea of being noticed and particularly liked the way Anil noticed her. He was not subtle. He looked for that second longer than everyone else and with an ease that came with practice. Monika felt comfortable with that. He was not a dirty old man who would drool within the comfort of marriage. He was honest. He liked what he saw and looked. He knew that she noticed him looking and that was fine. It was not vulgar. He knew that Monika appreciated his admiration.

'Really, or did Romala throw you out?'

'Haven't seen her for a while,' he said. 'Hope she is doing OK. What about you? What were you up to last night?'

'Wouldn't you like to know.'

The banter was usual, boring and didn't mean much apart from confirming the relaxed relationship Anil and Monika had shared for about two years. She knew he was lying about not having seen Romala for a while but because they had never met Monika felt no sympathy for her. It was as if Anil, despite his moral short comings, which Monika wouldn't have noticed even if she had taken the time to think about them, was closer to her for being a colleague than Romala.

'So what are you doing tonight?'

'Nothing much. Meeting Brian and Jo and a few of the others for a drink. You can come along if you want to.

If Romala hasn't promised you anything special tonight,' she said with a smile.

Romala hadn't.

'Yes, just might do that. The Slug and Lettuce is it?'

It was a place that they usually went to for a drink, a pleasant bar on the river with a terrace. He had never taken Romala there.

III

It was noisy at the bar. Everyone was there. It felt like an office reunion. As if spending a whole day with everyone was not enough or was it that no-one had any friends outside work. University was a long time ago and the world had become a small place. Small enough that is to enable everyone the chance of friendship.

Anil was late. He never liked getting there before everyone else. He needed the comfort of being able to move from one person to the next without having to find a believable excuse or being rude. He heard Monika almost as soon as he got there. Her laugh was free and loud as if to make sure that everyone would be in no doubt that she was already there. Anil took his time. He knew she knew he was interested. After all it was part of the game. If he seemed too eager she would lose interest. He also had to steal away to call Romala. He wasn't meeting her tonight but had promised to call. He got himself a beer, met half a dozen of his colleagues, made enough polite conversation so as to appear sociable and now had to meet Monika which was one of the more important reasons for coming. He enjoyed flirting with her. She was not easy. Not like Romala.

Anil worked his way to the balcony overlooking the river. It was a nice summers day. Hot enough for an excuse to meet up for a drink but not so hot that you would worry about having spent all day in the same clothes. His beer, which he didn't like, was warm.

'Hi Monika.'

'Hi, managed to get away did you? Did you finish the report.'

'Yes.'

Anil looked at his watch. It was nearly eight. Romala would be waiting for his call. He had moved in too quickly. It would take another half an hour if he had to move back to a quiet spot to make the call and get back to where he was in relation to Monika.

He had spent too long getting to Monika. Anil's enthusiasm had waned from the effort of trying to be inconspicuous about his attraction to her.

'Oh you poor little sour puss, been making you work too hard, Jeff picking on you again.'

'Stop being a cow Monika.'

'Alright, come over and say hello to Brian, he is the new Ops manager.'

IV

It was past ten before he left the pub. Kingston was quiet. Monika was still there but Anil was tired. He had a tough day ahead of him and needed to get some sleep. The night before had been an energetic one. At the thought of it he suddenly remembered Romala again. He had promised to call and hadn't. No big deal really, he thought, she should have got used to that by now. It wasn't that Anil deliberately ignored his promises to call her and knowing that was enough for him not to feel guilty. It was nearly eleven and Romala should have long stopped hoping that he would ring.

'Hi Romala, how are you?'

'Fine. Where are you?'

'On my way home. Look sorry I couldn't call earlier. Got tied up with work.'

'Oh, that's alright. Don't worry about it. Are you coming over tomorrow?'

He didn't know. He wanted to but only if he didn't have anything else on. He couldn't say that though. He wasn't that heartless.

'I'm not sure what time I will finish work. I'll ring you.'

It didn't occur to him that Romala might sit around waiting for his call. She always did even though disappointed after an evening of waiting for Anil to call or, on the off chance to actually come over, she would promise herself through tears that she would never do that again. Nothing changed. As always she found herself exactly as before, in the same chair, flicking through television channels and, in between odd telephone calls from friends who knew that she would be home, she would glance at the clock just to check how much her hope had faded.

Anil knew Romala to be a girl that liked staying at home. Romala had told him that several times so that now he no longer imagined that she might not like waiting for his call. In any event he was more concerned about keeping his options open just in case something more exciting came up, Monika, for instance. He didn't really believe it but offered it up as a 'for instance'. It was a pleasant 'for instance' to think about. He was sure Monika would be fun.

V

This wasn't going to be one of those relationships where the world would be offered an option to judge. Anil was not going to be a cad and Romala the unfairly done by maiden. They were both 'grown ups'. Both knew what the score was on relationships and the cost of maintaining them and both happy to pay the price. Romala had no illusions either. She liked Anil.

Romala had moved south to London as soon as she started University. Having lived in a sheltered Midlands community of Walsall she had already grown up a Hindu girl in the middle of a Muslim community where the rule seemed to be that as she was not a Muslim every Muslim boy could have a go. She had learned to cope with the sneers at school and the problems of being in a minority.

University had been her great escape except that she had soon found out that the prejudice was not solely a religious thing but more something born of human instinct. She had not put it into those words but understood prejudice as a way of life that she would have to ignore if she wanted to get on.

Anil was not only of the same faith but the same caste. He had invested a lot of time in getting her and she had willingly been worn down. In the end he wasn't bad. He certainly would have been acceptable to her parents had she the inclination of asking for their approval. She had been taken aback when he made his move to sleep with her. The surprise came not because she was still a virgin. She had lost that a long time ago with the naivety that still believed in true love being divorced from physical desire. No, her surprise came from the fact that she genuinely liked Anil and would have preferred if he had waited a little longer. He would be her third lover which in traditional terms was three too many. In fact in traditional terms she was already a slut if Anil had known. As far as he was concerned things never got sentimental and the relationship had not developed into the phase of exchanging stories about old lovers. As far as Anil was concerned Romala would cling to a modicum of good behaviour and confess that he was her second, the first having been a promise of love and marriage, in that order, forever.

Anil had been sweet, attentive, traditional, passionate, promising and she had accepted that as enough of a payment. It was fortunate that he was a good lover and although becoming somewhat absent minded of late was nice to have around. Anil had asked her to move in with him but that was too much of a jump for her to make. Anil hadn't been serious either. It was just on the spur of the moment in that 'after love making' daze when there was nothing to be said except that there still seemed the need for conversation. It was the thought of having to go home at an unearthly hour to get ready for work the next day that made him say it. He could have said that he wished he had brought a change of clothing so that he could go to work from her place in the morning but he didn't. He wanted dramatic effect and thinking of the immediate convenience of it asked her. He still had parents to answer to even though the divide of two hundred and fifty miles allowed him some privacy.

Marriage was of course not out of the question. Anil had not asked her but then had never ruled it out either. Religion was not a bar and neither was race or cast and Romala felt sure that having been together for nearly a year there would soon come a time when the inevitable would happen although, having said that, she was in no hurry. She had done well. She worked as a physiotherapist at St Thomas' Hospital in London, enjoyed her independence, and liked the fact that she had her own time. She was not ready to be the slave she had seen her mother be all her life. Not of course that her mother would ever admit it. Even when her father shouted at her, Romala's mother would reflect on the privileges marriage to a 'good man'. Romala knew that sooner or later it would happen. She too would fall into the trap of being an 'Asian' wife and although times had changed she would still need to observe the social rules that tradition had not yet given up. Anil would take his place in the status aspiring male dominant society that the Asian world still maintained within the fabric of English culture. A confusion of living in a hypocritical world where it didn't matter what happened outside the home so long as there remained the self righteous legacies of culture within the sanctity of the home.

Romala did occasionally wonder what would happen if Anil left her but having been through it twice knew the score......she would call in sick on a regular basis for a month until her supervisor would notice and suggest that she take a holiday. Romala would panic at the thought of having to spend all the time at home on her own, promise to snap out of it and then cry on and off for then next few weeks. She would enjoy the attention of her friends while being extremely careful not to over indulge herself on that score so as to lose them. Then after a suitable interval, and much coaxing of her friends she would then start going out again and inevitably meet someone who wanted to test his abilities as the great lover to lure an Asian girl away from the restrictions of tradition. The main thing was that Anil had not left her and as time passed they were getting used to each other. The more they did so it was her belief that things would become more permanent.

Anil didn't think it about the future much. He knew that his parents would as all good Asian parents find a virgin for him. He would then dump his old life for the pleasure of marriage that mimicked that of his parents. Until then there was always Romala and one should remember that there was Monika too.

VI

The next few days in the office were busy and Anil worked late. He lost interest in flirting with Monika and she went on to find another willing male in next to no time. A new girl from Accounts had interested him. He had used his bravado and asked her out. Sue, glad of someone within the company to show her the ropes, had accepted to his delight. They had been out a few times and he had even attempted an unsuccessful love making. Unsuccessful in that she was hard work and three dates later he had lost interest. There had been no relationship to acknowledge and therefore no need to break up. Anil and Sue were still friends and office gossip had been kept at bay.

Romala rang four times in three weeks, Anil once. Romala understood work had to come first. He didn't promise to come round and so by default didn't keep her waiting around the flat. Romala found the company of friends far less boring than she imagined and the fact that Anil no longer asked her to wait for his call gave her a freedom and light headedness that comes with knowing one has to entertain oneself and that it is not difficult. No moping around the flat or long soaks in the bath holding conversations with Ganesh.

'Hi Anil. How's work? Thought I would ring to see how you are.'

Anil was glad that she had called. He needed a break from working as hard as he had done these last few weeks and Monika was tied up at the moment. No new fish in the sea so a break was in order. At least with Romala he didn't have to work so hard.

'Glad you called. I was just thinking of you. In fact I was just about to call you. Listen, do you want to meet tonight?'

Romala didn't believe that he was thinking of her at that moment or that he would have rung her had she not telephoned but that didn't matter. Romala had called because she had nothing to do that evening. She missed Anil and hoped that he would call. He would call when he wanted to and although she had thought twice about ringing now that Anil was coming over she was glad she had. She was also glad that Anil didn't want to go out. A quiet evening at home with her was what she wanted and she was pleased that was what was on offer, another domestic one act play.

Anil came over a little later than he said he would but that was usual. Not a great cook Romala had bought some frozen Thai chicken on the way home which they both enjoyed despite the glare of the Hindu gods that decorated her sitting room.

He had bought some flowers. The absence had made the reunion more passionate. Romala enjoyed the extra attention that Anil paid her and Anil made an effort out of relief for being allowed into familiar territory again.

Ganesh was also pleased to see him the next morning.

VII

The next stage in the saga was expected. Anil's parents were coming over to visit. Inevitably the conversation would be on his agreeing to get married. After all he had a good job, was not a child anymore and they would come up with at least two prospective brides for him to check out.

The first was Sunita, twenty-six, a solicitor, of good family and of course beautiful. They all were! Her father was an accountant and had his own practice.

The second was Meera, twenty-five, an accountant, of good family and beautiful. Her father worked in a local branch of a bank.

They both were good professional girls of good Brahmin stock and it would be nice to have grandchildren.

Anil was dreading it. So was Romala. Both knew that a visit from parents bearing in mind the ages that they had reached would raise the question of marriage.

Anil had told Romala that his parents were coming over but had not suggested that he would try to introduce her to them. She knew that sooner or later Anil's parents would try and arrange a match for him and hoped that when that happened Anil would at least make an effort to introduce her into the selection process. He hadn't. He told her that they were coming to see relatives and hoped Romala would believe him. Romala wanted to believe him and did, so that when he said that he would not be able to see her for a few days she told herself not to worry.

Anil didn't call her as agreed. He didn't call to tell her that he had agreed to go and see the girls but not to worry. After his visits he didn't tell her that Sunita was the favourite although he did like the quiet, shy, Meera too. In fact he didn't ring her throughout the two weeks Anil's parents were in town.

It was during this absence that Romala realized that Anil had never talked of marriage. She had panicked a couple of times and on one occasion had telephoned him.

'Anil, do you love me?'

'Of course I do. I know it is difficult but it is only for a few days. They will be gone soon and then we will be together again.'

'Anil, I am scared. Do you really love me? I mean, do you

want to be with me? Will you always want to be with me? Tell me honestly, I'm scared.'

Anil was getting a little scared too. He did not want to be honest. He did like her. He enjoyed being with her but the thought of confronting his parents with a Indian girl who was living on her own, whom he had met in a bar was too much. The fact that he had been sleeping with her for over a year didn't come into the equation.

Anil knew his parents and therefore knew they wouldn't understand. They would never understand how it was that such a girl could ever make a good daughter in law. How could they ever imagine her living with them, looking after them, and most importantly being the sort of good daughter in law that they hoped for. She was, it was obvious, too modern he could hear his mother say. Not like the good Indian girls who had spent their time getting professional qualifications and then becoming obedient wives, good mothers and proud of looking after the home.

Romala had wanted a career. After all, she had left her family in Walsall to come to London for an education and stayed in London on her own. How could a career girl ever become a good wife? How would Anil ever convince them that a girl like that was still a virgin. How could they agree to their son taking on the responsibility of a wayward girl that had not had the decency of remaining pure for her husband to deflower! The 'how?' clichéd as the questions were, still mattered. It was not Anil at all but his parents that were the ones that needed convincing and Anil was not sure he wanted the hassle of it.

'Look, Romala, I've got to go now. I will ring you back. You are being silly. I love you and will come and see you as soon as I can,'

'Anil, can't I meet your parents. I am sure they will like me.'

'Sorry Romala, I have got to go. I will ring you later.'

Anil did ring her later. He was sure she knew what was happening. It was three days before decency required him to ring. He had already seen the candidates and had seen his mother and father off excited at having the future of their son to think about.

He had told his parents that he was not ready for marriage. He had probably told his mother at least a hundred times but still as his parents had already arranged the appointments he had agreed to go along. In fact in a strange sort of way he had enjoyed the visits. It was nice being the centre of attention. Of course, both girls were excellent cooks, and although professionals, knew how to keep house and understood the traditions which are required to contribute to a good Hindu household.

Anil had enjoyed entering the world of his parents. It was strange that here he was, born and brought up in England, living and working in London for the last three years and yet enjoying the experience of being in one of those over-the-top Indian films that he could not stand.

He liked Romala. She was nice but he didn't feel able to cope with the storm that would inevitably arise if he brought her up as a possible candidate. Both had shared protestations of undying love but there had been no promises made by either for the future. In fact he wasn't sure how Romala would fare in the face of the competition that had already been identified.

He didn't like the thought.

Romala did not reproach him for not ringing her back. She never did. She felt something was going on but Anil had assured her that there was nothing to worry about. Romala had nothing in terms of hard evidence to worry about and feelings are too hard to explain. She put it down to the monthly cycle which was the only believable reason she could come up with.

VIII

Anil didn't ring Romala immediately his parents went back. He wanted sometime to think. He had met both candidates and his parents had liked both of them. In fact he had joked with them about the idea of marrying both. His mother was not amused.

He had told Romala that his parents would be over for a few days and then perhaps a week. Now he told her that having stayed for two weeks they had extended for four. He used the extra two weeks to have a break.

He had thought about Romala during the process and wondered whether he ought to be fair and give her a chance. After all, the two new candidates, if Romala was the old one, had only vicariously promised him what Romala had already given him and the fact that he had his doubts about Romala's chances wasn't really something he needed to worry about. His conscience could then be clear.

He thought about how he would introduce her and decided that he wouldn't. He wasn't sure whether he didn't want to because it would be difficult to explain to his parents or whether he was more attracted by the idea of marrying a virgin. Of course he didn't put it like that in the arguments to himself. For him it was the question of how much of the past Romala had not admitted to him. At least with the new girls there was no experience to hide. Anil decided to stop thinking about it as the arguments were becoming more untenable.

When he did meet her he didn't think it appropriate to mention the real purpose of his parents coming over to see him. Just a visit to London. Romala was not sure whether she should believe him but as the evening drew on her doubts left her. They both nearly overslept and if it hadn't been for the increasingly noisy traffic as the morning got into rush hour mode they would have been late for work.

Monika was in good form, a little more cleavage than usual. She was obviously on the prowl.

'Hi Anil, haven't seen you around much.'

'Had my parents round but they have gone so you will be able to see as much of me as you want to. Fancy a drink?'

'You asking me out?'

Anil had not anticipated the question and now wasn't

sure of an answer. What he wanted to say was 'Well, as a matter of fact yes I am asking you out because I want to see what chances there are of sleeping with you. Your cleavage caught my interest. In fact I have been wondering what the chances were for a long time.'

'No, just wondered whether you wanted to have a drink,' said Anil.

'Alright, straight after work. Same place?'

It was clearly not the first time that they had been out for a drink so why should Monika suggest that this was a date.

It was agreed. Anil tried to forget that he had also told Romala that he would meet her that evening but he convinced himself that it would be alright. She wouldn't expect him until after eight so he had plenty of time. A drink or two, nothing more. If there was anything else on offer he would make his decision at that time. Why worry about it now. She was looking good. There was always a chance.

IX

Ganesh was feeling a little lonely. Romala knew he was as she lay in the bath staring at him. His eyes betrayed a living being that soap dish designers had conspired to obliterate. She wondered why someone would use a god to ornament a soap dish and was sure that Ganesh didn't like it. She remembered when she bought the soap dish. Her parents had a large statue of Ganesh at home and she was delighted at seeing a familiar face at an Indian discount store. Actually, all Indian stores were discount stores and although she didn't like them very much she found herself instinctively walking into everyone she passed. It must she thought have something to do with those weekly shopping trips with her mother that she grew up with. She didn't expect to get a Ganesh soap dish though. That seemed almost sacrilegious but then she liked it. It was nice to have a god in the most private place of all.

The water was getting a little cold. Romala added some hot water to the bath and enjoyed the sensation of the water caressing her body with increasing degrees of warmth.

Her thoughts moved to Anil. He was coming over and the long bath was a preparation for the event. She reminded herself that Anil loved her. She tried to remember when he had last said so and dismissed the struggle as soon as she found that she wasn't going to get an immediate answer. She reminded herself that she loved him. After all there was no hesitation in confirming that response.

She looked again at Ganesh. She wanted to pray. Lying there in the bath wasn't the right state to be in to pray but she didn't care. She tried to remember a hymn that her mother used to sing as part of her devotions. She couldn't remember all of it but at least she remembered the chorus. She sang in a soft sad pleading voice that seemed to be an underlying requirement of all hymns. Soon the soap dish disappeared and Ganesh took the form of the deity he was. She became more solemn in her devotion and soon she could sing no longer. She found herself crying, face buried in her hands and coughing out the 'please' of help.

The water was getting cold again so she ended the bath. It was almost seven-thirty and Anil had promised to be there by eight. He would be late as usual but she wouldn't say anything. She valued that extra time to relax. Not that Anil's visits were difficult. On the contrary Anil always took charge which meant that all she needed to do was to follow directions.

Romala was glad he was coming over. She wore a black dress that exuded promise and a little touch of perfume to complement the freshness of her body.

It was eight-fifteen when she next looked at the clock. He would be over between eight thirty and nine. She had decided on spaghetti with a green salad to start with and a nice bottle of supermarket wine. The Bolognese was done and just needed to be heated up. The spaghetti wouldn't take long.

Romala sat on the sofa and switched on the television. She flicked through the channels until through boredom settled on one. The program itself was of no interest. A discussion between two opinionated people who were certain there were viewers interested in hearing what they had to say about some conflict somewhere in the world.

X

'Sorry I'm late. Couldn't get out of the office. John insisted on being a prat!'

It was seven thirty by the time she had appeared and Anil was on his second beer and was already getting sick of the crisps.

'That's alright. No worries.'

A waiter came over almost as she sat down which was a lot better than for Anil who had waited for over ten minutes. Waiters did that sort of thing. It was part of the act of being gentlemen.

'So Anil, how's it going?'

The conversation was anything but dull. Flirting never is and Anil noticing the time didn't want to end the evening. If he got lucky it would be worth the effort of making it up to Romala.

It was past ten o'clock by the time Monika decided that she needed to call it a night. It had been fun and she was already a little drunk. Anil walked her to the station, decided it was too late for her to travel alone and would take her home. Anil was a little disappointed that Monika was not happy to invite him up to her flat but on the whole it had been a wonderful evening. The conversation was lively and the expectation of more than just a great evening provided the necessary adrenalin to relax.

It was too late to ring Romala but Anil did anyway. Somehow there was a comfort in their relationship that allowed him to do what he would not have dreamed of doing with anyone else. His phone call woke her up. Romala had fallen asleep waiting for him. She accepted his excuse of having to go to a leaving party and not being able to ring her any earlier. Romala asked him to come over. Anil had expected no less and was already on his way over to her.

Lying in bed that night with Romala cuddled up to him he stared into the darkness that allowed him to turn his thoughts to another life.

It was hard to choose. They were both pretty. They would both make good wives. His parents liked Sunita and they were right, she was the prettier of the two.

Anil hoped Ganesh wasn't listening.

*   *   *

Tarrantino Film

I

He was straight out of a Tarrantino film. Disgusting! The difference was that the film was art but this was not. This was real, a disgusting reality that smelled of vomit. I was caught. I was a fellow passenger. It was one of those moments when I wished I was travelling business class.

Affected politeness on his part was no more than deference to the accent my school had given me. His astonishment at my origin was a theatrical parody of human emotion enacted with determined exaggeration.

I had no desire to have a conversation with him but was forced by a natural courtesy which I have always retained. I cannot ape his accent either in the written or spoken form and therefore it is hard for me to give the reader an idea of the sort of person he was. I wish I could because the reader would then understand how a language can be reduced to a series of animal noises that communicate basic desire and no more. He boasted of his luck at ending a two week project that he had ended and got paid for without doing a stroke of work. A series of 'lucky' projects had enabled him to acquire a house in a 'posh' part of the town in which he lived. People thought he was lucky but they were stupid as far he was concerned because it was intelligence that made people lucky and intelligence had got him the good things in life.

He had a large house with four bedrooms, surround sound entertainment system, a wife that couldn't get enough of him and a dog. She was pregnant again, third time in five years. Stupid bitch, never remembered to take the pill. With pride he told me he had two boys that were going to grow up to be 'real hard nuts'.

His trip to a country in the former Soviet Union had enabled him to go 'ape shit' with his 'dick'. It was 'great'. He had met a girl that had not asked him for money. He had screwed her every day for the last week for two drinks a time. It was an 'effing good deal' he snorted.

Extraordinarily I continued to listen to him. He ordered wine depending on the colour of the meat that he was going to have and winked at me as he did so. He didn't think that one should not be sophisticated on occasion.

I am not like that at all. I dislike, as the reader has hopefully perceived, pretence. He was going to go home and take his dog for a walk and then see whether his wife still loved him. Another wink.

I cringed. The thought that such people existed in this world was unbelievable. That I had to meet them was what I know hell will be all about, mental torture without the option of slitting your throat.

I am already approaching fifty with everything worked out and achieved and yet I am not sure where I am going. I have had my mid-life crisis early and have been living it in silence for a number of years. There is nothing that I want more than anything else because I see the interference of mortality. I am more convincing in argument to others than myself because only I see through the intense futility of it all. Perhaps my reaction to this ape was partly because of that.

It was a four hour flight. I tried to imagine this as another of those experiences that one should have for the sake of saying one has had them. I tried to be interested, would have asked psychologically perceptive open questions, drawn him out as if it had been one of those business negotiations that were always good fun, aped sincerity, smiled when I should have and nodded in agreement whenever the question asked of me was rhetorical. But no, I wasn't given the chance.

Occasionally I was asked a question and after trying to answer it realized that the best solution would be to provoke him into patronizing me. Now that would be amusing, I thought, and for a very short time it was. Eventually I sought refuge in the in-flight entertainment system that dulled the senses to allow the secretion of time without effort.

We parted company on arrival. He had to rush because he had a connecting flight to catch. I sat glued to my chair trying to make sure that there was no way I would have to bump into him again.

II

I saw him once more on a flight from London. He changed his seat to sit next to me without asking me. I was ready with headphones and a book in front of me. Not reading it but remembering to turn the pages on cue. I saw him coming with horror and strained my attention on the page in front of me.

'Good book?'

'Not bad.' Damn! I forgot I had headphones on. I could have gone on ignoring him.

'What is it?'

'Kenneth Clarke's Civilisation,' I replied hoping that he would realize that we had nothing in common and leave me alone.

'What's it about?'

There are times when the simplest of questions is hard to answer. Not because you cannot but because you do not know where to start. If someone had said to me 'alright, you have 30 seconds to describe the book I could have done it. But he was serious and I think that is what threw me.

'About art and stuff,' I said trying to act as if I didn't really understand what I was reading.

'I don't know much about art,' he said, 'but I know what I like.'

That was it. He was not going to blaspheme. That was more than I could stand. A philistine that deserved more being tortured than just being put to death.

'Same here,' I heard the involuntary God of verbal spasms say.

'You don't remember me do you?' he said. 'I met you on the way to London in June. We sat together'.

'Oh yes,' I said imitating surprise in the same way he had when I had said I was from London.

'Yes, I got another contract. Six weeks this time. Am I looking forward to it! I am going to go ape shit when I get out there. I am going to show those locals what we are made of. Not like those sissy Italians or frogs. I have my phrase book and loads of cash. You wait till I get there. They won't know what hit them.'

Disgust.

'How was your trip home,' I asked trying the most 'open question' I could think of and for once the fates were on my side. As soon as he started I knew I wouldn't need to do anything other than timely nod, smile and use other basic body language that generally allowed ones mental faculties to go on standby.

'Oh it was great! Good to get good beer, hang out with my mates, shag a few slags.....'

I was losing it again. I scrambled around for help. Containing the anxiety in my voice I interrupted '....and your wife?'

'We're divorced.'

'I'm sorry.'

'No, I'm not sorry. Stupid bitch I am glad I am rid of her, threw her out of the house. She went to social services and those blood suckers got her a Paki solicitor. Couldn't even speak English.'

He suddenly came back. 'No offence.'

'None taken'. I was lying of course. It is amazing how people can be offensive and think that merely either asking to be excused or excluding the listener they can get away with it. I took offense not because of the colour of my skin but because I couldn't share in his prejudice.

'Yeah, but she didn't get everything. Sold the HiFi, tele and the furniture before she could get her hands on it. Left a whacking big mortgage on the place. She won't get a penny!'

I don't know why it took me so long but I suddenly realized that a family had broken up. I remembered he had children and they were young. Couldn't remember exactly how many but still I remembered. There was a wife without a husband and children without a father while this idiot was going to show those foreigners what he was made of.

I became sad. It was all I ever thought about nowadays, the inevitability of it. A feeling of self pity welled up inside me, a vacuum that caused physical pain. It took the twit shouting at me to snap out of it.

'You alright?'

Prat! Only he could ask a question like that. How the hell could I be alright if I were sitting next to him! I couldn't even ask to move for the effort that he had taken to occupy the seat next to me. He wanted to be with his long lost mate that he hadn't seen for ages. My eyes had pleaded not guilty but the old man moved looking at us as if we were made of the same mould.

'No, I'm sorry.'

'That's alright,' he said calling for the stewardess. She walked by switching off the call button with a seamless action that came from experience.

'My friend is not feeling well, could he have a whisky. Make that two.'

'The drinks trolley with be round in a minute, sir.' said the stewardess.

'I don't give a monkeys when the trolley's coming round. He doesn't feel good NOW. Get an effing drink!' he sprayed into her face.

The stewardess moved back in shock, recovered, looked at me as if to check whether I was in fact still alive and darted off with a 'Just a minute sir.'

'Don't worry,' he said 'Get you a drink in a minute.' as he turned to look down the aisle after her. 'She's a bit of alright. Show her a good time any day. Great arse' and turned to me.

'Not bad,' I said.

*   *   *

The Explanation

I

You know what I hate most is that just because I was out with friends until five this morning everyone thinks I'm a slut. That if I hadn't before I certainly now must have lost my virginity. I was just with friends. It was a birthday party. We sat around and talked. That was all. I didn't notice the time. It happens. But no, when I got home all hell broke loose. I had suddenly become this slut from hell. Christ! I am not out every night. I wasn't even drunk and believe me there was plenty of opportunity to be.

I played it cool. I worked it out on the way home. I would not take the bait. I wouldn't get angry. I would play the 'tired and not in the mood so I just want to go to bed' act. Thankfully my family does not practice domestic violence so I knew I would get away with it. I mean the bit about going to sleep. Of course I did not sleep. I listened to the hushed whispering next door.

II

'She is just like her father. Doesn't care a damn about anything. I just can't believe she would do something like this.'

'Has she done this before? I know why has this happened? She has obviously been drinking. She would be more responsible if she hadn't been drinking.'

My mother is a fine one to talk. All my life I've seen her getting drunk and being carried to her bed. No one complained. She was given ready-made excuses; had a bad marriage. Cruel husband left her when she was pregnant. All the clichés of a marriage gone wrong. I knew my father on the rare occasions that he decided to come and visit. Thinking that responsibility meant that he could come home when he had no where else to go. I knew my father. He was the one who came home like a dog who had lost a fight, his tale between his legs.... being extra nice because he didn't want to be thrown out.

He was once. It was when my mother had taken a new lover and thought that she had found the only man who didn't love her only for the cheap sex that she was so good at, stupid bitch. How she cried when he left her. He told her that she was stupid if she thought that he would spend the rest of his life with a drunken old hag. That was mean. I didn't find out what happened until two months after he moved out and she had to get drunk to tell me. Feeling sorry for herself she was.

I think she was enjoying it now. She always liked people feeling sorry for her. She had an audience now. Two sisters comforting her. It is not nice to be mean to someone in that state. Her sisters were enjoying the feeling of superiority. You know the feeling you get comforting someone who is totally exposed.

I heard them comforting her. They were just as bad. How pure they must feel.

'I just don't know what has got into her. She was such a nice girl.'

'Nice girl.' Amazing! But I don't really give a shit. They can think all they want to about me. I know I should not have stayed out late but I was having such a nice time. Didn't realise the time until it had gone twelve. I panicked when someone said that they had to go because it was so late. I almost rushed out of the flat but then I realised that I had left it too late. I knew was in for it. It would be one by the time I got home so I just decided to wait until I got a lift home. I worried a little as each hour passed by. It was nearly three-thirty by the time that someone offered to give me a lift home. Steve wasn't the one I wanted to give me a lift but then Mark had decided to flirt with Clara who was giving all the signs that she wasn't going to make it home without having to pay. I am sure she didn't. I got Steve. Thought he was in for a free lay. Got a surprise didn't he.

My mother started crying. God how I hated that. She

was good at it though. It was the only thing that she was good at apart from getting drunk and getting laid. Stupid bitch. I wish she would stop crying though. I hated that. God how she loved feeling sorry for herself.

'You are lucky. You've only got sons.'

It was alright to have sons who went around screwing left, right and centre. They were men. Men do that sort of thing. They can't help it. God! The logic made me sick.

I remember John. I am sure that he was gay. I remember him saying that every girl had a price. A price measured in compliments. He said that it never took more than five good compliments to nail a girl. Too right he was too. Five, the best of them only cost three. John was good. Good as any man can be. He was kind that's why I think he was gay. He didn't know it though. I imagined him going home and feeling sick about not getting any because he spent too much time being nice. I laugh but I feel sorry for him too.

The crying faded into a whimper. I was getting tired of straining to hear and decided to fall asleep. It would start all over again in the morning. I wouldn't miss much.

III

I lay there awake. I knew the inquisition would begin as soon as I got out of bed and was in no hurry to let it begin.

My mother came in and drew open the curtains. She didn't say a word. She was in mourning. The long-suffering saint. With the burdens of motherhood for all to see. I knew I wouldn't be able to last long. I wouldn't be allowed to sleep. My mouth tasted awful. I had to get up. I slipped out of bed as soon as she left the room. They heard me go into the bathroom. God I looked a mess. I had circles under my eyes. Seventeen years old and I looked thirty. It wouldn't be long before I turned into a hag like all the rest of the know-it-alls. I shuddered at the thought that one day I would be sitting in some room with all the comfort of thinking that I knew all the answers.

The mirror was dirty. Finger marks and splashes of water that had dried conspired to remind me of what a shitty life this really was. I knew I was being a bitch but they had it coming. I brushed my teeth with attention. I had to get rid of the taste in my mouth. The mouthwash bottle was empty, sitting there with the empty shampoo bottles.

I couldn't hear anything coming from the room next door.

IV

'I just do not know what has gotten into her. She was such a sweet child. I never thought that it would come to this. I have done everything I could. You know it is not easy being a single mother. I have worked hard, saved every penny and this is what I have got to show for it.'

'Don't blame yourself. It is not your fault. She was doing so well at school. She got 9 GCSE's and she was going to do well at her A levels. Her teachers said so.'

'She never wanted to go out with boys. Always so shy she was. When I tried to tell her the facts of life she didn't want to hear anything. What am I going to do.'

'Now come on Sharon. You can't go blaming yourself. You remember when she dropped out of school. She didn't tell anyone. She played truant for almost a month before those irresponsible teachers decided to do anything about it. And then they didn't tell you about it. Didn't come to you and say 'Well, Mrs. Simons, I am afraid that your daughter hasn't been to school for a while. We really ought to do something about it.' No, they didn't. They just sent a letter telling you that your daughter had been expelled. And what did she have to say for herself. Nothing! You cried for a week and did that make a difference. No! She sulked. Remember that she wouldn't even speak to us. She was so rude.'

'It's her fathers' fault. I told him that he had to own up to his responsibilities and all he could say was that I had got pregnant because I wanted to trap him. As if he had nothing to do with it. I relied on him to take precautions but he didn't. Then when I told him that I was pregnant he denied being the father. I was eighteen years old and what did I know, nothing! The last time he came back he lived like a lord, out of work, lounging about the flat all day, watching television. Stole money from my purse and blamed it on his own daughter, for a whole month doing nothing. I needed support. He would complain about being hungry but never helped with the cooking. It was only at night that he would be nice to me but I always knew why. When I really didn't want to he would call me names. I needed someone to talk to. That is why when Ron was kind to me at work I felt good. When he asked me out it wasn't like a date or anything. He was just someone to talk to. He listened. He cared about me. He was married and so was I. We were just friends. When we finally did it I did not expect it. I was a little drunk and he was gentle, at first. That is what took me by surprise. But it ended like all the rest; nothing special.

You know I didn't want to sleep with Ron. He got me drunk. I didn't want to. When I got home Harry called me a slut. It wasn't that late. I told him that I had gone to see Liz. He didn't believe me. Ripped my bag from me took all the money I had and left. I needed money. I asked Ron but he told me that he did not pay for it. I got an advance from work to tide me over.

Do you want a cup of tea? I'll make some'

V

'You know Dawn, I've always been ashamed of her. I always knew she knew she was a slut. She deserves what she gets. And now her daughter. She'll end up just like her'.

'What do you mean Alice? Don't be horrible to her.'

'Give it a rest, Dawn. She deserves a daughter like that, making out as if she is still a virgin. Do you really think that she hasn't already?

VI

The shower felt nice. I had scrubbed myself clean. It felt nice. All the dirt of the night washed away. The hot water massaged my skin to a smooth soft finish.

VII

The pleasure of the shower was coming to an end.

I realised that somehow things had to get back to normal. I would have to face them. The pain of having to face them alone hurt. I felt sick. There was an emptiness at the pith of my stomach. The vulnerable feeling that I had been hiding all this time became too much to hide. I didn't want anything yesterday. Just to spend a little time forgetting the shit that my life had become. There was nothing that ever went right. It wasn't fair. I didn't do anything.

Steve was going home. I asked whether he would give me a lift. He agreed. I was a little drunk but not so much that I didn't know what I was doing. Steve was OK but I didn't realise that everything had to end up that way. He stopped the car by the side of the road. We had been talking. He said he knew the way to my place so I didn't pay attention to the route he took. When he stopped the car I asked him what was wrong. He said he wanted a kiss. I told him to get lost. He leaned over and grabbed my breast. I pushed him away and called him the son of a bitch that he was. He hit me. I couldn't believe it. Grabbed my hair and pulled me towards him and tried to kiss me. I went mad. I hit him again and again until he let me go. I opened the door and got out. He swore at me, called me a tease, a slut leading him on.

I was crying. I ran away from the car and turned a corner. I hid behind a garage wall looking to see whether he would follow me. He didn't. I waited a few minutes to make sure. My lip hurt. The bastard had cut my lip. It hurt. The tears fell down my face. I licked the tears on my lips and felt the sting. It was almost four. I didn't know where I was.

Alone, and I looked a mess. I was angry and frightened. It took me a while to get a hold of myself. I don't know how I got home. Two night buses and a long walk home. They were waiting for me. I knew they were coming over but I didn't think that they would stay to gloat. My mother was so stupid she didn't realise it. She thought it was pity. She didn't think that they were merely reassuring themselves of how much better off they were. God, how people enjoyed living in the gutter; useless people who lived their useless lives which meant nothing to anyone.

I hurt. The pain had moved lower. I almost cried out. Five years I had hurt every month. Every month for five years! I sat on the toilet and waited for the spasm to pass. As I doubled over I watched the colour of the water turn red. It was time. Still a virgin I bled the dirt that was the sign of womanhood.

VIII

I came out of the bathroom. I didn't care what they would say. I went to my room and changed into something that wouldn't give me away. When I came out my mother was standing there.

"Good morning sweetheart. Do you fancy a cup of tea?"

*   *   *

The Voyeur

I

The world is a strange place. Full of happenings that are
so close to you that they remain unnoticed. Yet with all
one can say of that unfortunate sense of being closeted in
a private make believe world it is by some magical revela-
tion that they unexpectedly become apparent. A revela-
tion born of an insignificant event which, by its very innocence, creates an acute discomfort that tips one over the
edge just enough to lose control for a moment. It is of such
a occurrence that I have had a great desire to tell someone
for the last few weeks that now, in the middle of the night
when sleep should recreate the body for another day of
living, I switch on the computer and begin to write.

What I promise is not another love story. We all know
there have been enough of those. I do not intend to add
to the myth propounded by so many over the years that
there is in this world something that goes by the name
of love that drains us of so much energy when the reality is that all one has to show for it is a memory which
is rarely accurate. I am going to tell you of a world that
many of the faith to which I belong find a more pleasant
but transitory experience to that of the pain and fruitless
pastime to which the rest of the world so happily sacri-
fices so much.

II

I saw her serve at table with a grace as young as it was
involuntary. Her body had developed unexpectedly and
you could see her mind trying to catch up. She knew what
it was that she had to do. She knew how to stand and
stare until the craning neck of the diners had lodged their
exasperated faces into every private space she moved. She
served and cleared the tables with an indifferent smile that
left her thoughts uninterrupted by the constant passing

glances of customers taking a break from idle conversation.

I saw the others too. Each had a different style of working but they all carried themselves with numbness. The others warranted a short span of attention, the sort that one gives to clichés, wonder and then nothing. No epitaph required. But she was different. Her long length uniform covered the movement of her hips and legs, her waist, her breasts. Seemingly hiding them from any improper thoughts that I could have had but I suppose she could not have counted on the vividness of my imagination. I knew what they tried to hide. Each little curve suggested by movement I was able to extrapolate due to the long experience of seeing what I wanted to see. Her hair, a pleated ponytail reflected her form. No idle revolution here. No renegade hair escaped the pleats in her hair.

The customers were the same. Couples affecting affection, businessmen in suits that had required more attention than the subject matter of their conversation. They were misfits who enjoyed the scene created by others but I was alone in longing for nothing to happen and nothing did. The god of my own creation I dissolved conversations into white noise and I drowned into a stupor that eliminated all thought of the fact that I was on my own because there was no one else to be with.

Loneliness is not something that comes to those who seek it. Like an unwelcome guest who comes and goes as he pleases it intrudes in those most vulnerable moments in life that generally desire anything but that emotional reaction. I, who had been alone before walking into the restaurant, was now among the multitude each striving to entertain me.

She came around again, my little darling, another little tour of the tables, eyes and hand working in unison, a mind on automatic pilot. I noticed her fingers as she removed the plates on which the dishevelled remains of what I had ordered were taken away. No nail polish. It must be a rule. No nail polish to distract the customers or was it hygiene? Still, they were delicate fingers; long and fleshy morsels that could be kissed, nails clean and manicured, hands still chubby. Remnants of the child left behind by the maturing youth I had before me. I was able to steal a glance before she left. Trained to notice I received a smile. I lingered in my gaze to send the message of the flirt and hoped it would be received as special interest. She noticed that too and gave me an extended smile in reply, which I thankfully used to warm my heart.

She brought me the bill. I paid it without checking whether it was correct leaving a tip to make sure that she would remember who she had served. The arrogance of the customer that suggests what you do counts with other people because it is special for them; a gift that means more than just a tip from another customer. She would remember me not from the special customer recognition training that she had received but from the warmth of my custom. I was special for honest reasons.

I left the restaurant pleased with myself. I had had an afternoon affair without complications and she was there for me to return to whenever I wanted to indulge myself.

III

The air was fresh and the clouds cheated by the sun allowed my face to be warmed by the winter air. The impatient Saturday traffic sped around me busily gathering up food and drink and energetically spending before the week of toil began. I walked to my apartment leisurely transforming a ten-minute walk into fifteen. I had a cup of coffee when I got home because there was nothing else to do. It was still only two o'clock. Taking a book I left the silence no more than half an hour after entering it. I walked round the block to a park where I chose a park bench away from the other afternoon strollers. As it was still not the season for park escapades it was relatively empty but a man of my experience did not need crowds. A magician, I could conjure up fantasies with a sprinkle of reality to last a lifetime. An hour or so was merely child's play.

There were the old usuals; an old couple that did not have the means to dash around on shopping expeditions, single pensioners who were getting used to being alone after a lifetime of depending on programmed certainty, small groups of men impatiently discussing the world before time ran out and among them, pigeons, staining paths in search of morsels on this warm winter's day. I knew which ones to pick on immediately, two boys about fifteen years old, too young to smoke but nonetheless laying the foundation for the excesses of later life. They were serious as only young people can be; talking intently about the uninvited intrusions in their lives, about parents, teachers, school, and uncertain futures. I knew which ones were being discussed today by the seriousness with which they spoke and agreed. Well, obvious really to someone with as many years of eaves dropping as I had.

In that moment of self-indulgence I lost my concentration. I forgot the golden rule of the game I was playing; one never observed unless one's mind was totally on the subject. One of the boys looked up and noticed me. I let my gaze fall naturally to the book open at any page. I smiled inwardly at the subtlety with which I could do that. I kept my eyes on the book for a few discreet moments and then looked up again. They were both now returning my stare. I had lost the game. I didn't mind. I did what one always does in such circumstances. I turned to my book and started reading. The words happy at my renewed attention started to make sense, talked to me, took me away from the embarrassment that would otherwise have drowned me. I didn't look up again until I was sure they were no longer there. They weren't. I went home.

IV

Saturday was coming to an end. It had been a relatively good day. I remembered the good lunch, how I had enjoyed the walk, the fresh air and the book that I had so long used as camouflage. The loneliest part of the week was about descend on all unsuspecting souls who found themselves not already having made the commitment that provides the safety net of routine.

I was a little hungry and knew that before long I would feel the pangs that would make the rest of the evening unpleasant. Low blood sugar levels had the effect on me of accentuating every sad emotion I had. I decided to eat again. Lunch had been fun but I couldn't go to the same place again. The faith required me to change the venue so that I would remain invisible. I picked a little restaurant that had in the past offered me the diversion I needed.

V

It was a small restaurant. About thirty tables which, although arranged at a discreet distance from each other were still close enough to allow conversations to be overheard. I took a favourite table strategically placed to see the bar and all the tables without much effort. The waitress came over and I ordered a drink. I was in no hurry and therefore took my time to study the menu in search of something that might be different from my usual order. The drink was the waitress' suggestion because she had remembered my order from previous visits.

There weren't many customers. It was still early. I ordered a salad to start with and told the waitress that I would order the main course depending on how I felt after I had had the starter. She was not entirely happy but with the numb tolerance that I have come to expect smiled and walked off.

She was a plump girl and as she walked away I reminded myself of how her skirt covered her ample bottom with an affection that only just allowed the hips to move so that she could walk. I smiled at the thought of how much difficulty she might have if she had to bend down or indeed sit. Her shoulders were shaped so that straps fell into a comfortable dip just below her collarbone and her back looked as if it had the few extra pounds that made her bones lie comfortably at night. Her hair just off her shoulders had not been indulged more than a quick few strokes of the brush and so was unremarkable. My gaze moved on.

A new arrival, he sat three tables diagonally across me on his own. I couldn't tell whether he would remain on his own through the evening. He had a face about forty years old but looked older in experience. Confident and successful he was the sort of person who did not worry about being on his own. Sharp lines leading up to his cheekbones setting off eyes that revealed a little lack of sleep. Perhaps this was the start of another adventure or another conquest that would add to the darkness that cradled his eyes.

Another arrival. A couple this time. Not young enough to allow each other the curiosity that demands attention throughout the evening but still enough for terms of endearment.

My salad arrived. My waitress had changed. Perhaps it was the disinterest that my waitress had felt at having to go to the trouble of taking an order that was only half done. I wasn't sure why that had happened and wondered whether the waitress who now served me my salad would know about me wanting to order the main course once I was done with the salad. I asked. She did. My original waitress would take the order for the main course. She was just delivering my salad.

I ate slowly. The restaurant was filling up. The quietness of the restaurant was slowly building up to the chorus that is the mark of every successful establishment. New couples arrived. Groups became larger turning couples into foursomes and foursomes into groups of five and six. The waitresses were now speeding up in their delivery. Eyes darting about them trying as hard as they could to avoid the desperate gaze of customers yet not as successfully as they had been while I was the only one in the restaurant. Three new waitresses had joined the two that had received me. That made five to watch with an increasing number of customers. Even though I was eating slowly there was a moment when I knew that the salad was not going to last for ever. I was losing interest.

I pushed away the plate and waited for someone to come and take it away. It was funny how when I didn't care anymore the service became efficient. The waitress came and took the plate away and asked me whether I wanted anything else. The manner in which she asked me would not have enticed me even if I had wanted something. I asked for the bill. I paid and left.

VI

A light drizzle had started to fall while I was in the restaurant and was there to greet me as I walked out. I stood there for a moment not knowing what I wanted to do. I didn't want to go home. There was no one there. I had made sure of that by allowing two near commitments in my life to fail. The last of those commitments had ended over a year ago. Actually, nearly thirteen months ago. Since then I had kept away from every offer of a better acquaintance to ensure that I did not make the same mistake again.

It started raining a little harder. I decided to turn home and walked slowly making sure that I was not hurrying home where I knew I would be faced by another half hearted decision to do something simply because there was nothing to do.

"Oi you! Pervert!"

I turned just in time to feel the venom of the punch that felled me to the pavement. I don't remember much after that. Perhaps a little of the pain I felt as I was kicked while lying on the pavement.

VII

Next I recall waking up in hospital with a doctor asking me what had happened. I told him I didn't know. He turned away with that annoyed look that you get from someone who is angry at your utter insensitivity for his feelings. I couldn't help. I didn't know. I was discharged without the kindness of spending a night in the hospital.

VIII

It was as I awoke the next morning that I remembered you. I knew that you were watching me. I had felt the intensity of your gaze all week. I didn't know why you had done that to me. I didn't mean anything by it. All I wanted was the companionship of your presence. Not with me but close. Close enough to hear your hair dance in time to your walk. Too see you smile, the sound of your voice, the pleasure of our souls as they entwined and despite the crowd of customers not one would notice and in all of this you would never have to do a thing.

I felt the sense of betrayal as I understood what had happened. It was a familiar feeling. I had felt it twice before.

*   *   *